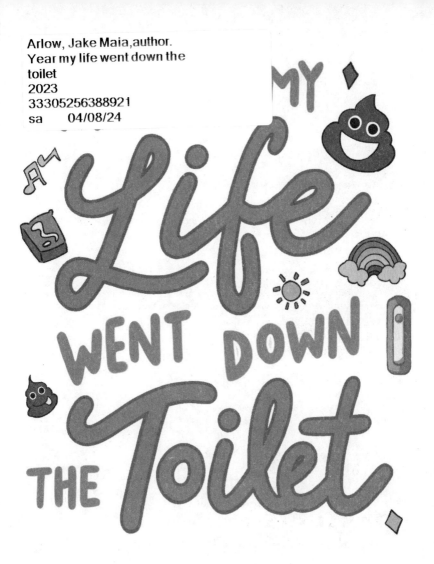

MY Life WENT DOWN THE Toilet

JAKE MAIA ARLOW

Dial Books for Young Readers

Dial Books for Young Readers
An imprint of Penguin Random House LLC, New York

First published in the United States of America by Dial Books for Young Readers,
an imprint of Penguin Random House LLC, 2023

Copyright © 2023 by Jake Maia Arlow

Visit us online at PenguinRandomHouse.com.

Library of Congress Cataloging-in-Publication Data
Names: Arlow, Jake Maia, author. Title: The year my life went down the toilet / Jake Maia Arlow.
Description: New York : Dial Books for Young Readers, [2023] | Audience: Ages 10-14 years. |
Summary: Twelve-year-old Al, short for Alison, navigates an overprotective mother, growing apart
from her best friend, and her first girl crush, all while her recent Crohn's diagnosis puts a knot in
her stomach. Identifiers: LCCN 2022054231 (print) | LCCN 2022054232 (ebook) |
ISBN 9780593112960 (hardcover) | ISBN 9780593112984 (epub)
Subjects: CYAC: Crohn's disease—Fiction. | Coming out (Sexual orientation)—Fiction. | Lesbians—
Fiction. | Friendship—Fiction. | Middle schools—Fiction. | Schools—Fiction.
Classification: LCC PZ7.1.A7475 Ye 2023 (print) | LCC PZ7.1.A7475 (ebook) | DDC [Fic]—dc23
LC record available at https://lccn.loc.gov/2022054231
LC ebook record available at https://lccn.loc.gov/2022054232

Printed in the United States of America
ISBN 9780593112960

2nd Printing

LSCH

Design by Cerise Steel
Text set in Macklin Slab

To Dr. Haller for letting me be your patient until I was a full-grown adult walking around the pediatric gastroenterology wing of the hospital.

And for all the kids with IBD. You're not too much.

Chapter One

AN UNFORTUNATE GURGLE

Some "scientists" claim that everybody poops.

Which *might* be true, but I have a hard time believing it.

I'm not saying I want to see some proof, because that would be disgusting. But if everybody poops . . . how come no one talks about it?

And even if everybody *does* poop—which, as I mentioned, I don't believe—I'm pretty sure no one on Earth *thinks* about pooping as much as me. Not because I want to think about it—I don't. I'd rather think about anything else, such as being mauled by a walrus or having my face eaten by a bunch of tiny cute mice.

But the problem is, my body *makes* me think about it. My stomach hurts *all the time*—at home, at school—and especially during gym class.

I wish that my brain didn't have to be attached to my body. Having flesh and bones and arms and legs and intestines is the cause of almost all my problems. If I were just a brain in a jar connected to a supercomputer, I'd never worry about having stomach pain or pooping or doing something embarrassing. No one would be able to tell if I was a kid or an adult or someone with a messed-up stomach or a normal one. No one would be able to tell if I was a girl or a boy or maybe something else.

But I'm not a supercomputer, so I have to run laps.

"Do you think the Addisons sweat at all?" That's Leo. He's not a fan of gym either.

We've been walking around the track for like fifteen minutes, and at this point my pit stains have pit stains.

All the other gym classes got to stay inside today, but Mr. DiMeglio used to be a professional wrestler, so he's really hard on us. He doesn't care that it's a hundred million degrees on the track.

"No, definitely not," I whisper to Leo, watching as the Addisons—Madison and Addison—lap us for the second time. "They're robots."

Madison and Addison (yes, those are really their names, and yes, it's annoying) are best friends, and they're both super athletic. They never post pictures on IG without each other, and all their posts get a ton more likes than everyone else in seventh grade, and sometimes more than people in eighth.

Leo and I are not friends with the Addisons. We're pretty much only friends with each other.

"Wanna know what my Italian teacher told us last period?" Leo asks as we walk to the outermost lane of the track to let everyone pass us.

"That you should've taken Spanish with me?"

He rolls his eyes. "No, he said it's the language of *opera*." Leo turns to me and grins, and then, when he's sure no one's listening, he imitates an opera singer, arms outstretched. "*CIAO, MI CHIAMO LEOOOOOO.*" He sings it so that only I can hear, and I can't help but laugh.

"What does that even mean?"

He slips his hands into his khaki shorts' pockets. He never changes for gym if he can help it, and I don't blame him. I always wear shorts or sweatpants and a T-shirt on gym days and then swap whatever shirt I wore to school for a baggier, dirtier one that hides my body.

"It means 'Hi, my name is Leo,'" he tells me. "It's the only thing I know how to say in Italian so far."

We both lose it at that, giggling so hard that we have to stop walking.

"Leonard! Alison! This isn't the mall! I want to see you jog!" Mr. DiMeglio shouts at us from his lawn chair. Yup, his *lawn chair.*

Leo and I cringe. Neither of us likes our real first names—we're Leo and Al, thank you very much, but Mr. DiMeglio never calls us that.

I swing my arms a little so it looks like I'm jogging, but Leo *actually* starts jogging, so I run to catch up.

"I hate him," he mutters. "'This isn't the mall'? Who says that? What does that even *mean*?"

"Don't listen to him," I tell Leo. "Remember when they fired him from Positive Youth Development for being too negative?"

Leo shrugs, but he keeps jogging. After a minute he asks, "So, did your mom make you that doctor's appointment yet?"

I look behind us to check that no one heard. "Not here," I whisper, then run ahead, even though the bouncing makes my stomach clench. Because we can't talk about this in public.

I've had stomach problems for a while, but they got really bad last winter. I tried to hide them from my mom, except she saw how often I was in the bathroom, and now I have to go to the most embarrassing doctor to ever exist (a *poop* doctor—yup, you read that right) even though I'm basically fine. I didn't want Leo to find out, but my mom told his mom, and now he knows, through the mom-gossip grapevine.

After a minute of running in silence, we somehow get lapped by the Addisons *again*. And that's when it hits me.

First, there's the gurgle. Next, there's that *feeling*, the one where all I can think about is what's happening in my intestines. I want to stop jogging, or maybe scream, or just not be on this horrible, too-hot track in the first place.

I try to hold it in. I try, I try, I try. But I don't think I can. I skid to a halt and dig my fingers into my hands and groan because what am I even supposed to do? I don't have time to run inside the school to get to a bathroom.

Leo turns to me, his eyes wide. "Do you need me to do anything?" He must realize what's happening even though I've done my best to hide my emergencies from him.

DiMeglio blows his whistle and shouts something at me as I shake my head at Leo, because I'm beyond help.

Then I see it: a porta potty off in the distance.

I take off. The only thing that exists in the whole world is the porta potty on the other side of the track and my messed-up stomach on this side. I'm sprinting, running faster than I ever have in my life.

I fling the porta potty door open. It smells like rotting garbage, but there's nothing I can do about that. I rush to put toilet paper over the seat the way my mom taught me when I was little.

Then: relief.

Pure relief.

For, like, two seconds.

Before I realize what just happened.

My entire gym class watched me run into a porta potty. A PORTA POTTY.

I have to drop out of school. That's my only option.

I guess I *could* say I threw up, because for some reason vomiting is less embarrassing than pooping. I bend over and put my head between my knees as a particularly painful bout of *you-know-what* happens.

I wish I could jump into the porta potty.

But I know it'll get worse the longer I stay in here, so as soon as I'm done, I pump some of the gross old soap residue onto my palm and walk out into the bright September day.

Everyone's huddled together by the edge of the track. I walk over as quietly as I can, hoping no one will notice me, but as I make my way to the edge of the group, Mr. DiMeglio looks up and says, "Glad to have you back, Alison," and the Addisons whisper to each other and start giggling.

Gym class should be illegal. I wish I had hopped into the porta potty when I had the chance.

Mr. DiMeglio tells us that we're running the mile next week, and Leo leans over and whispers, "You all right?"

I stare at the yellowing grass.

"I don't wanna talk about it."

Chapter Two

MY KISHKES

"You *sure* you're okay?" Leo asks as we walk home from school later that day.

Gym is the only class we have together, so he hasn't seen me since The Incident.

"I'm fine," I tell him. I'm really not, but he doesn't need to know that. It's bad enough that he knows about my stomach problems in the first place. "But can you *promise* not to say anything to either of our moms?"

He looks up at me—and he has to look waaay up, because I'm a full head taller than him—and puts his hand on my shoulder. "Yeah," he says. "Promise."

I smile at him, relieved. At least Leo has my back, even if my mom doesn't. She's convinced I have a "real problem," when the cold hard truth is I'm just a kid who poops a lot. It's fine. I'll go to this special doctor and she'll fix me up and I'll never have a porta potty emergency ever again.

Leo and I only live a few blocks from school, but my back's already sticky with sweat from carrying all the giant books we need for seventh grade.

I'm debating just letting my backpack crush me so that I never have to set foot in our school again when Leo asks, "Did you see the club flyers in the hallway?"

I snort. Leo and I aren't club people. "Yeah, I saw," I tell him. "Who would want to be in the *Ice Cream Crew*? What do they even *do*?"

"Maybe they go out for ice cream?"

"This is why we don't need stuff like that," I say, putting a clammy hand on his shoulder. "We can get ice cream on our own, just the two of us, and we don't have to deal with other kids or the teacher advisors. I bet they don't even let you get sprinkles."

"I guess." Leo shrugs. "But maybe we could join *something*. I'm sure not all the club people are like the Addisons."

"No, some of them are like *Duke Waters*, who's even worse."

(Duke set the boys' bathroom on fire last year during a Model UN competition.)

Leo shakes his head. "I don't know, maybe there's a club that could be fun for us to join together."

"We have a club," I tell him. "It's the Al and Leo Club, and it meets daily in your bedroom."

I should probably mention that Leo and I live together. Not, like, *together* together. But we live on the same floor of the same building. Which is kind of incredible, because I'm like ten feet away from him at all times.

But the best part of living in the same building as him is

that our apartments are directly above his mom's bakery, so it smells amazing *all the time.*

"I like our club," Leo admits.

"See?" I tell him, hiking my brick-filled backpack farther up on my shoulders. "That's the only group we need."

We arrive at our building and open the door to Klein's Kosher Bakery, and we're blasted with cold air and the scent of Jewish desserts.

"Well, look who it is!" Leo's mom, Beth, says from behind the counter.

She washes her hands and runs over to give Leo a hug and a kiss, and then she pulls me in for a hug too.

People in the store always mistake me for Beth's daughter, probably because we're both white and Jewish and tall and lanky and have light-ish brown hair. (Honestly, sometimes I wish she *were* my mom. She's funny, she bakes, and she doesn't ask me about my stomach.)

But people never randomly guess that Leo is Beth's kid, which makes all of us super mad, and no one more than Leo. He looks more like his dad, who is Filipino and lives in New Jersey—he's short and chubby and has light-brown skin.

"Can I interest you two in the challah nub?" Beth asks.

Leo turns to me and grins, and I fake a grin back. Normally, I'd be super excited about the challah nub—the end of the challah that she doesn't turn into French toast or sandwiches—but today my stomach hurts too much to even think about eating.

"Yes *please*," Leo says, and Beth brings it out for us on a paper plate.

"But save your appetites, okay?" she says before she hands it to us. "We're having dinner together tonight."

"*All* of us?" Leo and I exchange glances. We usually have dinner in our own apartments with our own moms. Sometimes we'll light Shabbat candles and have dessert together, but, yeah. Dinner is separate.

"Yup!" Beth says, and her smile gets too big.

"Why are you being weird?" Leo asks.

"Not weird," she says quickly. "We just thought it might be fun! Celebrate the first few weeks of the school year, that kind of thing."

"Okay . . ."

Luckily, a customer walks in, and we're spared any more of whatever that was. Leo perches on a stool at a small café table with the plate, but I tug on his shirt and usher him over to the stairwell before he gets too comfortable.

The fire door slams shut and drowns out the bakery sounds and smells, and we plop down on the concrete stairs.

"Why can't we sit down there and eat?"

I look at the plate of food, and my stomach makes an audible gurgle.

His eyebrows scrunch up. "Are your kishkes still hurting?"

"A little," I say, but my *kishkes* betray me by gurgling again. Leo calls them that because it's what Beth says; it

10

means "guts" in Yiddish. "But it's fine, you eat it. I'm not hungry."

He gives me another look as he takes a bite of the nub. I wish I *could* eat it. Leo's mom's challah is my favorite food. It's fluffy on the inside and salty on the outside and it melts on my tongue (well, it does when I can eat it without needing to run straight to the bathroom).

"Why do you think we're having dinner together?" Leo asks.

"Maybe the landlord raised the rent again?" That's happened before, but it's not usually a group discussion. I don't tell Leo that I think it's because of my stomach. That maybe my mom is going to try to have an apartment-wide talk about how sick I am and how everyone should try to be extra careful around me. She'll tell them they need to make sure I'm eating the "right" things, like you'd do with a baby when they have too much mush and spit up all over themselves.

But I'm not a baby; I know how to take care of myself.

"What if location scouts came by and they decided our apartment was the perfect place to film their movie?" Leo asks, getting excited. "Remember when they did that at the Main Street theater?"

I nod and laugh a little, but I don't think that's what this is.

When the Hollywood people came to our town, Leo freaked out. He was practically bursting with excitement, and he forced me to go down to Main Street with him so we could casually stroll by the film set. He thought maybe if we walked back and forth enough times, one of the casting directors would spot him and shout *YOU'RE PERFECT!* and make him the star of the movie. But when we were a few blocks away from the set, he chickened out and we ran back to our apartment and ate day-old cake instead.

"Do you wanna practice the song later?" I ask, changing the subject. Just thinking about what this dinner could possibly mean is making my stomach hurt. "We could play it for our moms tonight."

"Yes!" He jumps up from the stair he was sitting on. "We *have* to."

Leo and I do this thing where we write really weird songs and perform them for our parents. Well, Leo performs. I sit in the background and play my ukulele. He's too shy to talk in class, but he's amazing when he's singing for our moms. I don't like to be in the spotlight, but I love being Leo's backing band, so we're the perfect duo.

The only place we ever play our songs is in our apartments. You couldn't pay me a trillion dollars to perform at the school talent show or something like that. It would be like having a big sign over my head that said LOOK AT ME AND JUDGE ME!

I know Leo feels the same way, like how he didn't want anyone but me to hear his opera singing on the track even though he's actually pretty good.

"Ecretsay andshakehay?" Leo asks me as we climb the

rest of the way upstairs to the hall between our two apartments.

"Ofyay oursecay."

He just asked if I wanted to do our secret handshake, and I said of course.

Leo and I taught ourselves pig Latin last summer so that we could talk about whatever we wanted without our moms picking up on it. We mostly ended up talking about YouTubers, but it's nice to have the option.

Our handshake starts off with a double high five, then we grab each other's hands and cross them. Next, we release them with an explosion sound.

Leo jumps and points to me. "Al!"

I point to him. "Leo!"

We wrap our bent index fingers around each other and say "Arrrr" (because they look like pirate hooks when they're crossed like that).

The grand finale is lifting our entwined fingers toward the sky and shouting "MATEYS FOR LIFE!"

We're both a little out of breath after doing our handshake, grinning at each other. Maybe our performance will help Leo forget about my stomach stuff.

"Meet in your room for rehearsal later?" Leo asks. "I just have to do some homework."

"Sounds good."

We wave goodbye, then head into our separate apartments, only feet apart. It's the best of both worlds: He's close when I need him, but we don't share a bathroom. It's comforting to know that Leo's just across the hall.

When I walk into the living room, my mom's watching TV on the couch. She pauses it when she sees me and gives me her undivided attention, even though I'd prefer if it was a little more divided.

"How's your stomach feeling today?"

"Fine," I tell her, crossing my arms.

I can't believe *that's* the first thing she asks when I come home from school. Actually, I guess I *can* believe it, since all she's been able to talk to me about since my stomach started hurting is, well, my stomach.

She stands up from the couch and takes my backpack from me, letting it fall onto the floor near the kitchen table.

"I can do that myself," I mumble.

She must not hear me, because after she's done she asks, "Want a snack?" as she opens the fridge. "I got you some plain applesauce from work. I read on this cute little blog that it's easy on the stomach."

I shake my head. "I already had some challah," I tell her, even though it's a lie. I don't need a special diet just because my stomach hurts. I can eat what I want.

She frowns. "Are you sure that's good for you?"

I shrug and make an *I don't know* sound in the back of my throat.

"You don't want to hurt yourself more by eating the

wrong things," she says, and when I shrug in response yet again, she *tsks*, which makes me want to scream.

She's being all, "Oh, Al, do you need applesauce?" or "Oh, Al, here's this food tip I saw from a post on Facebook" (Facebook!!) or "Oh, Al, I saw on a YouTube video that nuts give you diarrhea, so I picked them out of your salad."

Maybe when I go to the doctor, she can fix my stomach *and* calm my mom down.

"I'm going to my room," I tell her.

But of course, before I can settle in, my stomach clenches and I run to the bathroom.

It's a relief to be completely alone and to sit on the toilet for as long as I want. Sometimes I rest here until my feet get all tingly from being in the same position for so long. It sounds weird, but it's almost better to just stay put so that if another wave hits, I'm already where I need to be. When I'm done pooping, I flop onto my bed and rest on my stomach, which is the comfiest position for me. Even once I've pooped out most of the pain, it still feels better.

It's also the perfect position to scroll through TikTok for hours. My mom doesn't *technically* let me have social media, but she doesn't check my phone.

The TikTok I'm scrolling on now isn't even my main one. This is my TikTok that no one at school follows or knows about—my secret backup account—where I watch what I actually want without the Addisons' dancing videos ruining my algorithm.

My For You page is a mix of stuff, but it's mostly videos

of girls who like girls. It's kind of wild that TikTok knows I want to see those kinds of videos, because that means it knows I feel the same way.

That I like girls, I mean. That I have crushes on them. It's not a big deal, but I don't want to tell people. Not even Leo. It's one thing to have my stomach hurting all the time and be sick or whatever the doctor's going to tell me, but I don't need my best friend to know about my random crushes too.

But on my backup TikTok, I can be someone else entirely. I can be my full queer self, and comment on girls' TikToks, telling them they look cute or that I like their outfit, even if the outfit is just a giant thrifted sweatshirt with an embroidered prairie dog on it. None of them know about my stomach, they just know I'm queer like them.

It's not that I'm trying to hide any of this from Leo, it's just that it would be weird to talk about people I might *like* like with my best friend. Saying I'm queer would mean telling Leo that I know I like girls. That I know I get crushes at all. That I want to kiss someone (eventually).

I think that would be embarrassing even if I were straight. It's better to just keep it in, to live life like the supercomputer without a body that I aspire to be.

I scroll through TikTok for a few more minutes. I'm exhausted from the day, but my brain is too focused on school and cute girls and the storm happening in my stomach for me to fall asleep.

It's possible that seventh grade will be the worst year of my entire life.

Chapter Three

THE SQUEEZING HAND OF DOOM

I must've fallen asleep, because I wake to my mom knocking on my door, telling me that it's time to head over to Beth and Leo's for dinner.

Her hair is wet and she's wearing makeup, which is *so* not like her that I have to fight the urge to laugh.

It's not that hard to "head over," because Beth and Leo's apartment is three steps away, but I tell my mom I need a minute. I figure if my mom's wearing *makeup*, then I should put in a little more effort than showing up with post-nap hair and a rumpled T-shirt.

"Can you grab this?" My mom hands me a loaf of bread once I'm changed and in the living room. "We're having turkey sandwiches."

"That's it?"

She smooths my hair down and looks me over. "It'll be easier on your stomach."

I have to stop myself from rolling my eyes. Leo always tells me about the delicious dinners Beth makes for the two of them, like salads and stews and brisket. I thought since we were going over there, we'd have something like that. But of course my mom wouldn't want me to eat something that actually tastes good.

I stay a few steps behind her as we walk across the hall to their apartment. She opens the door without knocking, which is completely weird. Even *I* knock on the door, despite the fact that Leo has told me a million times to just come in.

"We're here."

"Kitchen!" Beth calls out.

Leo's putting napkins and utensils on the table, and my mom and I hand the sandwich materials off to Beth.

"Idday ouryay ommay elltay ouyay at'swhay oinggay onyay?" I whisper to Leo. Translation: *Did your mom tell you what's going on?*

Leo shakes his head. "Onay," he whispers back.

That one's pretty self-explanatory.

When the table's all set and we sit down to eat, Beth lets out a long sigh. "I'm so glad we could have dinner together today."

"Me too!" my mom says, and she has on that same too-big smile that Beth had earlier.

Before we eat, Beth has Leo recite a prayer over the sandwiches.

He shifts a little in his seat and glances up at me before saying super quickly, "Baruch ata Adonai Eloheinu melekh ha'olam hamotzi lehem min ha'aretz."

I turn to my mom, who meets my eye. We barely know what the blessings are for, let alone how to say them. We're not that religious, though we sometimes welcome in Shabbat with Beth and Leo.

We all say amen even if we don't all know what we're saying amen to. Then we dig in.

Except . . . I don't. My stomach's been feeling this way all day—like whenever I see food, something down there knows there's too much else going on for me to even try to digest. I know that if I take even one bite of food, my stomach's going to do something horrible. It's like there's a giant hand squeezing my intestines. So while my mom and Leo and Beth take big bites of their blessed turkey sandwiches, I nibble the crust and try to look busy.

"So," Beth says in a serious tone, and I know that whatever she's about to say is the reason we're all here. "We thought it would be a good idea if the four of us have dinner together more often."

"We live across the hall from each other," my mom adds quickly. "We should be spending more time together."

I meet Leo's eyes, and he grins. "Sounds good to me."

"Me too," I say hesitantly.

"Great!" Beth says, looking relieved. "This'll be fun."

"We could even play board games!" my mom says, even though I don't think she's ever played a board game in her life.

So . . . that's it? I don't know why Beth and my mom were acting so strange if they were just going to say they want the four of us to hang out more. I had thought they were scheming, which is my and Leo's thing, not theirs.

After that, the giant hand squeezing my intestines lets up a bit and I'm able to eat most of my turkey sandwich.

Once everyone's done, Beth grabs us dessert—some leftover apple pie that didn't sell at the bakery today—and we sit back down to eat. Leo doesn't take a single bite though, which is weird because apple pie is one of his favorite desserts. Now that I can eat, he can't.

No one talks for a few minutes while *most* of us enjoy Beth's pie.

But then my mom asks, "So how was school?" because she always picks the moment my mouth is at its fullest to ask questions.

"Fine," I say quickly. I don't add anything about what happened in gym.

Leo kicks my foot, but I still don't mention The Incident. His eyes are pleading, and I try to communicate to him that it's all good and under no circumstances should he worry about me.

"Yeah, fine," he tells my mom. "I saw some signs for clubs, and . . ."—he meets my eye, then quickly looks away—"I don't know, I was thinking about doing drama club."

I snort a little, because obviously that's a joke. Leo's too shy to perform in front of anyone but me or our moms.

"I'm serious," he says, staring at his pie slice.

"Oh."

The hand squeezing my stomach is back, but it's more than that. It's like the squeezing hand also decided to punch me while it was at it.

"I think that's great, bubs," Beth tells Leo.

"I do too," my mom says, and she smiles at Beth.

I try to get Leo to look at me again, but he's concentrating really hard on his apple pie slice. I'm just trying to figure out what's going on, how he could do something like this when he couldn't even sing fake opera on the track without making sure he wasn't overheard.

Things are majorly awkward for a second, but then Beth starts talking like Leo didn't just drop the biggest news of the century; news he didn't even bother mentioning earlier when we were talking about clubs.

There's an even stronger pang in my stomach then, and I know I'm having another emergency, like the one I had in gym.

"I, um . . . I need to go—"

I run out of the room. My mom calls out after me, but I can't stop. The panic rises in my throat, and I want to cry.

So when I make it to the bathroom in my apartment, I do.

I put my head in my hands and let it out.

It's like my stomach doesn't know how to handle everything that's going on in my life. Especially not Leo deciding to do something like drama club, something that I would never do with him. That he *knows* I would never do but wants to try anyway.

When I get off the toilet, I go straight to my room. My whole body hurts, not just my kishkes.

After a minute, there's a knock on my door.

"Al?" my mom calls.

I don't answer.

And the worst part is: Leo and I never even got to debut our song.

Chapter Four

LITTLE AL'S GOTTA GO

Every other Saturday morning, you can find me and Leo eating our weight in semi-stale rugelach and watching old episodes of *High School Musical: The Musical: The Series* while we wait for his dad to pick him up.

We grab all the stuffed animals from both of our beds that we probably should've outgrown years ago and make a huge, cozy pile to watch the show. I've been trying to pretend that things are normal since the other night when Leo announced that he wanted to join drama club and *I* promptly ran away to poop and cry (in that order).

Leo turns to glance at me every once in a while, looking up from the episode playing on his phone. I purposefully avoid turning toward him—I'm worried he wants to talk to me about drama club.

But once we settle into the show a bit more and relax our shoulders into each other's, everything feels almost okay.

After the episode is over, Leo packs his weekend bag and we wait for his dad in the bakery.

"You gonna be okay while I'm gone?" he asks. "Like, with the bathroom?" He hasn't checked on me like that before, but now that he's seen my gym-class emergency, there's no going back.

"I'll be fine," I insist, reaching for a raspberry rugelach to prove it. I take a bite and it's buttery and jammy and perfect, even after sitting out for a day. My stomach will be mad at me in a few minutes, but I don't need Leo worrying about me for the whole weekend.

And once I see the special doctor, he won't have to. We can go back to being Al and Leo without stomach stuff or drama club (hopefully) or anything else to ruin it.

Eventually, the door jingles and Leo's dad walks in. Any worry that Leo was feeling for me falls from his face as he grins and throws his arms around his dad.

"Hey, iho," Leo's dad, Alec, says as he wraps Leo into a hug. He looks over at me and waves. "Hi, little Al, how's it going?"

"Pretty good, big Al." It's a joke we have, since both of our nicknames are Al. It's nice to have an inside joke with Leo's dad, especially since I only really see him when he comes to pick Leo up or on special occasions. The two of them have a million inside jokes, since both Alec and Leo are hilarious. Leo told me about one where whenever either of them says the word *surely*, like, "Surely the rain will stop soon," the other says, "Don't call me Shirley!" (It's funnier if you say it out loud. Or maybe it's not really that funny if I have to explain it. Anyway.)

I like having something that's just mine and Alec's. It makes me feel like I'm part of Leo's whole life, even if that's not *necessarily* true.

Beth comes over from behind the counter and ruffles Leo's thick black hair. "Don't forget to start your English assignment."

Leo groans. "That's not due for like two weeks."

"But don't you still have to read the book?" Alec asks.

Leo looks over at me and rolls his eyes. I roll mine back in support, but there's something about seeing his parents talk to each other in that way that makes me feel a whole mess of emotions, all of which—surprise, surprise—make my stomach gurgle and ache.

Leo's parents might be divorced, but they get along super well. And Leo's dad knows everything that's going on in his life even though they only see each other every other weekend and some holidays.

My dad, on the other hand, is some random guy named Shelly who lives in Rancho Cucamonga, which is in California. I only found this out last year when my mom sat me down to have the "Dad Conversation" that she'd been promising to have for approximately my entire life. She told me that she had had something called a one-night stand, which is when you only meet someone once and then get pregnant. (Well, I don't think everyone gets pregnant from a one-night stand, but my mom did. And that's how I came into the world.)

My mom told me that if I wanted to try to reach out to

him I could, but I don't. He's not a dad like Alec. He's just some guy.

Leo runs back over to me to grab one last rugelach. "Text me how you're feeling, okay?" he asks, and I nod.

But I'm not going to, and I know he won't check in on me. We don't talk much when he's at his dad's house, because he's always having too much fun with the other side of his family.

I've asked a few times if I could go with him for his weekend sleepovers, but Beth always tells me that it's just Leo and Dad time. Which I completely understand, obviously, but I wish he didn't have to leave me for two whole days twice a month. On the plus side, though, he always brings me and Beth back ensaymadas from his dad's cousin's Filipino bakery. They're soft and cheesy and sweet and almost make up for the fact that I have to endure two endless days without Leo.

Before he goes, I tap Leo's shoulder. "Ecretsay andshakehay?"

He nods and reaches out his hand, and we do a silent version of our secret handshake that we came up with for when we're out in public. Then Leo leaves with his weekend duffel bag and his dad, who loves him more than anything in the world.

It's the saddest part of my week, when I have to watch Leo walk out that door.

Before I know what's happening, my stomach twists along with my heart, and I'm running to the bathroom.

I don't want this to be my life anymore, one that I spend either running to the toilet or on the toilet or worried about the next time I'll have to have an extended stay on the toilet. And hopefully, if the doctor's appointment goes well, it won't be.

Chapter Five

NOW I HATE WINNIE-THE-POOH

Everyone at the children's hospital is too nice. The doctors and nurses smile these huge smiles at me like I just learned how to recite the alphabet for the first time. The person at the front desk even asks if I want a sticker. A *sticker.*

I mean, fine, I do want it, but only so I have something new to put on my water bottle. I want to text Leo about how they're all smiling at me like creepy clowns (we're both terrified of them), but I don't want to bother him while he's with his dad. He's only been gone for like a day and a half, but I've stored up about a billion things to tell him now that it's Sunday evening.

My mom taps her foot as we wait to take the elevator up to pediatric gastroenterology, which she does when she gets nervous, which makes *me* nervous.

Eventually, the elevator arrives, and we make it to the third floor. The Pediatric Gastroenterology and Nutrition suite has giant glass doors and signs talking about how they're the best place in the country for kids who poop too much.

Okay, it doesn't actually say that, but that's the gist of it.

My mom lets the person at the front desk know we're here, and after a few minutes a nurse in Winnie-the-Pooh scrubs comes to take my vitals and bring me to the examination room.

Then, we wait, and wait, and wait, and—

"Alison?"

I nod at the person who just walked into the room, my legs bouncing as I sit in a chair that's meant for much smaller kids. "Um, it's Al."

"Al, hi! I'm Dr. Maltz." She reaches out her hand to me before she says hi to my mom, which is pretty cool.

Eventually, I reach my hand out too, and she smiles at me. I have to admit that it's a nice smile.

"So, what's going on?" she asks as she washes her hands and sits in front of her computer.

"Well, I've noticed that Al—" my mom starts, but Dr. Maltz interrupts her before she can embarrass me completely.

"I'd actually love it if *you* could tell me what's going on, Al," she says, smiling at me again. My cheeks get hot, but this time I smile back at her.

"Can you talk about your symptoms?" Dr. Maltz continues. "For instance, when did they start?"

"I guess since the beginning of the school year," I tell her, avoiding my mom's gaze. She made this appointment after noticing I was going to the bathroom a lot, but I don't want her to know *all* the details. "I'm really fine, though," I add. "Like, it's nothing serious."

Dr. Maltz smiles a bit at that. "How about you tell me how you've been feeling. Is it any different than it was before the start of the school year?"

"Well, like, my stomach's been hurting a bit more," I admit. "And also I've been going to the bathroom a lot and stuff like that."

Dr. Maltz nods. "That must be really tough."

"Um, kind of?" I don't want her to tell me it's tough. I *know* it's tough, I'm the one who almost pooped my pants at school. I just want her to fix what's wrong so I never have to talk about my butt again.

"And when you go to the bathroom, is there ever blood in your stool?"

My eyes almost pop out of my skull. "Stool?"

"Your poop," she says. "Just a fancy word for it."

"Um, yeah," I tell her, because there almost always is.

"What?" my mom asks, her eyes wide with horror.

I shrug, because I sort of figured that was how everyone's poop was.

Dr. Maltz just nods and closes her computer. "Can you sit up on the examination table for me, Al?" she asks as she pulls on a pair of blue gloves. "And Mom, would you mind stepping outside? I'm going to check out Al's stomach, and our middle school patients usually like to do this in private. Is that all right, Al?"

I nod as hard as I can, because oh boy is it all right. Thankfully, my mom leaves without any comment and I jump up onto the table.

"So, Al," Dr. Maltz tells me. "First, I'm going to press on your belly. It won't hurt, just a little pressure so I can feel what's going on in there. And after that I'm going to ask you to pull down your pants so I can do a rectal exam."

My stomach clenches just thinking about that. The thought of anyone seeing me in my underwear (and then my naked butt) is almost too much to handle. "Will *that* hurt?"

"Well, I'm going to have to do a digital exam, which means I'm going to use one of my fingers to check to see if there's any blood."

I'm about to pass out from embarrassment. Seriously, my body's just going to shut down. Dr. Maltz is going to have to touch. My. Butt.

She's looking at me expectantly, though, so after a minute I take a deep breath and lie back on the exam table. Dr. Maltz starts by pressing gently on my stomach as promised, and it's like a massage until she presses down on a tender part.

I make a face, and she asks, "Did that hurt?"

"A little," I admit.

She nods. "Okay, Al, now can I ask you to pull down your pants and underwear a tiny bit for me, and then turn on your side?" She must notice the sheer panic on my face, because she adds, "I see butts every single day. It's my job. And I'll do my best to make it really, really fast."

I pull my clothes down, wishing more than ever that I was just a floating brain with no body.

Please, let me become invisible, I think as Dr. Maltz does something . . . uh . . . well . . . super gross . . .

She puts her finger up my butt.

If anyone at school found out about this, I would have to infiltrate the next rocket launch and flee the planet.

When she's done, she takes the gloves off and washes her hands. I avoid her gaze.

"So, there was blood," Dr. Maltz says once my mom is back. My intestines gurgle at the words, and I'd like to be anywhere else in the entire galaxy.

My mom frowns, and looks over at me with pity in her eyes. "What does that mean?"

"It could be nothing, but it's usually a signifier of disease. I'm going to schedule a colonoscopy so we can find out what's going on for sure." She looks over at me. "A colonoscopy is when we use a tiny camera and snake it through your intestines to take a look inside of you. It's like *The Magic School Bus*, if you've ever seen that."

I nod. I'm doing a lot of nodding today, but only because there's a lot of information being thrown at me and everyone's talking about my butt and I don't know what else to do.

"What do you think it is, though?" my mom asks.

"Well, I can't say for sure until we see the lab results from the colonoscopy, but I would guess probably something under the umbrella of inflammatory bowel disease, most likely ulcerative colitis or Crohn's disease," Dr. Maltz says. "We can talk more about that if that is in fact the diagnosis."

The diagnosis.

I'm going to have a *diagnosis*. That word sounds way too official. I don't want my poop to require a diagnosis.

Then again, if there *is* a diagnosis, then maybe there's a cure for everything I'm experiencing, and I just need some medicine or a little rest and relaxation and then I'll be fine. No poop emergencies on the track, no stomach gurgling or diarrhea or Olympic-level sprints to the toilet.

Dr. Maltz is about to leave when she says, "Oh, and I just wanted to let you know about our middle school IBD support group that happens every Wednesday here at the hospital." She hands me a pamphlet. "If we find out that that's what's going on, I think it would be a great resource. It can be really helpful to talk to people who are going through the same thing as you, so you know you're not alone in all of this." She hands me the pamphlet, her smile too bright for the words coming out of her mouth. "Plus, I'm pretty sure some of the kids from the group go to your school!"

She says that last part like it's a *good* thing. Like I would ever want to talk to other kids from my school about poop.

"Um, thanks," I say.

But no thanks.

Chapter Six

A SQUELCH TO END ALL SQUELCHES

In the few days since my doctor's appointment, I've tried to put Dr. Maltz and her pretty smile and evil finger out of my mind, but it hasn't quite worked.

When Leo got back from his dad's place, we didn't talk about my appointment or drama club. He told me about the movie he watched with his dad—some old musical from the "golden era" of Hollywood.

"Everything was so glamorous back then," he told me. "They just don't make films like that today."

I looked down at my giant T-shirt that had a faded picture of a dolphin from a trip my mom took to Florida when she was a kid. "You're saying this isn't glamorous?" I asked Leo, and we both laughed at that, and the awkwardness kind of went away.

Kind of.

Now, though, we're in gym class, and I'm being extra careful, because until my stomach gets fixed, I'm not risking any more porta potty excursions.

"I want to see you all kick as high as Addison here," Mr. DiMeglio shouts, pointing to Addison's leg. She's holding her heel so that she's in a perfect standing split.

I roll my eyes and then look over at Leo, who rolls his back.

We're doing a dance unit in gym, but DiMeglio is only having us work on kicking today. "Your legs are your foundation," he told us. "Strong legs equal a strong body."

The whole class is standing in the middle of the gym, spaced out enough so that we don't whack each other in the face. Leo and I are at the edge of the group, as far away from other kids' legs as possible.

"What do you think the other gym classes are doing right now?" I whisper to Leo.

"Probably something normal like dodgeball."

"Lucky them."

"I want to see those legs in the air," DiMeglio shouts to the group.

"Are we catching up with our friends tonight?" I ask Leo after a minute.

That's our code for watching all the videos our favorite YouTubers have uploaded since we've last seen them. We joke that they're our friends, since it's not like we have any others.

"Definitely," he says, kicking his leg half-heartedly. "But can we also watch the recording of last year's school musical?"

"Why?" I ask him, kicking my leg with even less enthusiasm.

He shrugs. "Just for research."

My stomach gurgles the way it did last time he brought up drama club. I'm still not convinced he's serious. It could all be some big joke and on the day of auditions he'll be in his bedroom like usual and we'll laugh and watch YouTube videos and do what we normally do, just Al and Leo. Together.

Leo and I continue kicking in silence for a minute. The Addisons and some other girls are wearing leggings that show off the shape of their thighs. I'm wearing the loose knee-length shorts I wear on most gym days, since we're not allowed to wear jeans. After my colonoscopy is done and my stomach problems are fixed, maybe I'll feel comfortable in my own body like the Addisons. Not that I'd want to show off my thighs, but at least I wouldn't want to throw myself into a well and never come out.

I keep kicking even as my stomach grumbles more and more. I tell myself that it's fine, that it's just getting jostled from the physical activity.

Until there's a sharp pain at the bottom of my stomach. I double over, waiting for it to pass.

Leo rushes closer to me. "What's going on?"

"Nothing," I tell him as the pain migrates from my stomach to my butt, making it nearly impossible to kick without everything hurting.

"Alison, where's that big kick?" DiMeglio shouts over as he wanders through the gym correcting people's form.

I glare at him, and gear up for my highest kick yet to prove that I'm just as good as Addison, even with my stomach in knots.

And then, as I fling my leg up, something happens. It feels like a fart but . . . more solid.

Oh no.

When I bring my leg back down, there's a squelch.

NO NO NO. This is *not* happening.

I need an asteroid or a large piano to fall directly on top of me so that I don't have to deal with what I'm pretty sure just happened.

I reach my hands behind my back to cover my butt, walk as fast as I can to the edge of the gym, then push myself into the girls' locker room.

I feel like a literal baby who can't control when and where they go to the bathroom. But it's worse because babies have diapers. I have cherry-patterned underwear that I bought with a gift card I got for my birthday. And now they're ruined.

When I make it to one of the stalls, I quickly strip down and assess the situation, trying to peel my shorts off without letting the poop leak out of my cherry underwear. I stand there for a minute, staring in horror at the mess I made.

This is the end. I can't face the outside world after this.

I pinch my nose shut, but then I can't breathe because tears are flooding into my mouth.

"Al?"

Oh no.

It's Leo. In the girls' locker room.

I don't respond, squeezing my eyes shut and waiting for him to leave. I can't have him anywhere near me while I'm like this. What if he *smells* me?

"Al, are you okay?" he asks, getting closer.

I grab my underwear and frantically throw it in the little trash can in the stall so that at least the evidence is gone. But then I instantly regret it because there's still half a day of school left and I'm going to have to go commando.

"Should I go get the nurse?" Leo asks from just outside the bathroom stall.

"NO!" I shout. "Please, Leo, don't."

"But didn't you, like . . ." Leo doesn't finish the sentence, but I know he's asking if I pooped my pants.

"That's not what happened," I say, my voice not sounding like my own.

"I just wanted to make sure you're okay."

I'M NOT, I'M NOT, I'M NOT, I want to scream.

Instead, I take a deep breath and say something I never thought I'd say to Leo. "Can you go?"

"What?" he asks.

"Can you *leave*?" I yell.

I'm standing in the bathroom stall, trying to figure out

how to get out of this situation alive. "You shouldn't even be in here."

"Um, okay," he says, clearly hurt. He takes a deep breath, then walks away.

I shake my hands out and whine, clutching my stomach. I didn't think things were this serious. I thought this *problem* might go away on its own.

Or maybe that's just what I wanted.

Instead, I made my best friend angry, ruined my nicest underwear, and had a real accident for the first time since I was in diapers.

So, half-naked and covered in tears and probably traces of my own poop, I sit down on the toilet and finish what I started with my high kick in the gym.

Chapter Seven

THE WORDS **MIRACLE** AND **LAXATIVE** DO NOT BELONG TOGETHER

"**I did some** research and it says that if you can't control your bowel movements, that's a sign that something's wrong," Leo says from where he's sitting.

We're both leaning against the foot of his bed, scrolling on our phones. It's been a day since Gym Class Incident Number Two (which also happened to be . . . a number two), and Leo won't stop talking about it.

"Nothing's wrong," I tell him firmly. Sure, I've had a few poop events that have been less than ideal. But my colonoscopy's tomorrow, and everything will be all right after that. Dr. Maltz will be able to cure whatever's going on and my life will go back to normal.

"I'm just saying that I'm worried," Leo says. "If you have to poop so badly that you go in the gym—"

I put my hand over Leo's mouth. "Please don't."

Even though there's no one around to overhear our conversation—our moms are out right now, seeing a movie—I still don't want him to finish that sentence.

"So do you think our moms are, like, best friends now?" I ask Leo, changing the subject. "Has your mom said anything else about all of us hanging out more? You know, since the dinner."

"Yeah, she talks about it all the time," he says. "And my mom's always texting yours. She sends her these ancient memes of cats with that big blocky text. I don't even know how she finds them, because she's not on social media."

I laugh at that. "That's so weird."

"I know."

Maybe now that my mom's texting and hanging out with Beth more, she won't be as focused on me and my stomach and what I'm eating.

I'm so glad she didn't find out about my gym . . . uh . . . explosion, but I do wish there was an anonymous poop hotline or something. Like, some number I could call and talk about my stomach stuff without them ever having to see my face (or butt).

It's fine, though, because after my colonoscopy, none of this will be an issue.

As if he's reading my mind (or maybe just very concerned about my stomach), Leo asks, "When do you have to start getting ready for your intestine camera thing?"

"It's a colonoscopy," I tell him. "And not till early tomorrow morning. But I have to stop eating tonight."

He turns to me. "Are you gonna have to wear a hospital gown?"

"I don't know." I shrug. "Probably."

"What about those grippy hospital socks?" he asks, sounding... *excited*? "My dad got to wear those when he had his gallbladder removed."

I shrug again. I don't care if I get to have grippy socks, because someone is going to *stick a camera up my butt.*

The more questions Leo asks, the more he sounds like my mom, and I hate that. He's the person I go to to get away from her, and if he's just going to be pestering me about my stomach and all the "cool things" I'll get to do in the hospital, I'd rather be in my own apartment, alone.

"I think I actually have to go," I tell him, standing up so fast that I see multicolored spots in my vision.

"Oh, okay," Leo says, also standing up. "Text me tomorrow, okay?"

"I will," I say, even though I don't plan on it. He'll be at school while I'm pooping my brains out.

Maybe a colonoscopy would be slightly more tolerable if you could just go to the hospital the day of and have the procedure and be done with it. But no, you have to *prepare* your body, and that's what's completely horrible.

Let me tell you about the world's worst torture method: MiraLAX.

So basically, it's this medicine that's normally used to help people poop if they're having trouble with it. I guess it's a combo of the words *miracle* and *laxative.* But I'm

100 percent sure the person who named it has never had to drink one full bottle of it within the span of a single afternoon.

I've spent most of the day trying to guzzle down the laxative without throwing up, then running to the toilet to poop. So now I'm curled up near the end of my bed, scrolling through TikTok like my life depends on it.

The MiraLAX will be worth it when Dr. Maltz checks out my intestines and tells me how to cure my, uh, excessive pooping. At least, that's what I said to myself as I held my nose and gulped down the horrible sludge.

I'm catching up on some of my favorite TikTokers' videos; the creators are this really cool queer couple. One of them has purple-and-blue braids and wears combat boots and always has perfect winged eyeliner, and the other has electric-red hair and wears tops that her girlfriend crochets for her. I want to be just like them when I'm in high school.

But I don't think I *can*. Neither of them has to run to the bathroom all the time. Neither of them is about to have a colonoscopy. Well, as far as I know.

I wish my life were different. I wish that my stomach was normal and that my mom wasn't always worrying about me. I wish that I could have a cool queer aesthetic and post videos on TikTok where people commented how they wished they were like *me*. I wish I could stop caring what people like the Addisons thought of me.

I wish my backup TikTok could be my main one. I wish

my backup *life* could be my main one, the one where I watch videos of girls who are dating without needing to hide it, where Leo and I make up songs without him wanting to join drama club. One where everything just feels easier.

Except nothing is easy. With the colonoscopy and my poop emergencies, that life feels so far away.

And so does the bathroom. Because today is just one emergency after another.

The worst of my "prep" is over, but every once in a while, I still have to run to the bathroom to finish clearing out my bowels.

"You feeling okay?" my mom asks as she pops her head in before walking into my bedroom.

I shake my head. I'm too tired to lie.

"My poor baby," she coos, rubbing my back as I flip over and bury my face in my pillow.

Normally I'd be mad about her talking to me like this, but right now it's nice. I feel so helpless, so empty from the laxative and so worried about what the colonoscopy will be like. I tried watching a vlog about someone's colonoscopy experience, but they were a grown-up and they had already had other procedures for other grown-up problems, like cataracts and hemorrhoids. I've never even broken a bone.

I'm almost asleep from my mom's calming words and back-rubbing, when my body betrays me.

Because once again, I have to poop.

"All right, sweetie, we're going to roll you in in a minute, okay?" the nurse in the colonoscopy suite tells me. Then she turns to my mom. "She should be out in about half an hour, give or take."

I look over at my mom, who smooths my hair back and plants a long, hard kiss on my forehead. There are tears in her eyes, which freaks me out. So I start crying too, because what if something goes wrong and I never see her again?

Like last night, her doting doesn't feel like overkill. It hardly feels like enough.

"Wait, Mom?" I ask before the nurse rolls me in. "I, um, love you," I tell her through tears.

"I love you too," she says, her voice breaking.

The nurse smiles at both of us and undoes the latch on the hospital bed, rolling me into the procedure room. "I'll take good care of her in there," she tells my mom. Then she says to me, "You'll fall asleep, and then you'll wake up and it'll be over. Easy-peasy."

The room she rolls me into is large and white, with lots of beeping machines.

"Ali!" Dr. Maltz says. She's standing by a big TV and reading some paperwork.

"Hi." I wave weakly.

"Do you feel all cleared out?" she asks, and I nod, because the MiraLAX did its job. "Great." Then she says something to the nurse that I don't really understand, about the placement of the IV.

"Are you comfortable, sweetheart?" the nurse asks.

"Mhm," I tell her, even though I'm about as far from comfortable as a person could be, on a hospital bed in a bright room, about to be knocked out and have a camera shoved up their butt.

"I'm going to administer the anesthesia now," the very bald and very buff anesthesiologist tells me loudly.

Tears stream down my face. I can't help it. I don't want them to force me to go to sleep.

"Will it hurt?"

I've already asked that like ten times today, but I still have no idea what they're doing to me. Maybe this is what an alien abduction feels like.

"It might itch a little as it goes in," the bald guy tells me. "But I'm going to have you count backwards from a hundred, and I promise you by the time you get to ninety you're going to fall asleep, okay?"

I nod, tears and snot dripping down my face. The nurse smooths back my hair, and the anesthesiologist connects my IV to the anesthesia drip.

"Here we go. Start counting . . . now."

But instead of counting, I scream.

"IT HURTS," I choke out. "IT HURTS."

"One hundred," the nurse says calmly. "Ninety-nine—say it with me, hon."

My vision turns into a tunnel. My veins feel like they're on fire, like my blood went away and was replaced by poison ivy.

"Ninety-eight."

"Where's my mom?" I ask, but my voice sounds far away.

Then the nurse says, "Ninety-seven."

Then, there's nothing.

"Hey, Allie." My mom smiles at me. She's holding on to my arm with tears in her eyes.

"Did they do it?" My voice is small, and my stomach hurts, and I'm back in a big room with other hospital beds. "What time is it?"

"It's all done," my mom whispers. "You did so well."

"It's done?"

"They finished the colonoscopy, baby," she whispers. "You're waking up now."

The nurse comes by and hands me water and pretzels, but all I want to do is sleep. My body is shaky and I'm so, so tired. I let my mom rub my back as I curl up on the hospital bed. The slow circles calm me down and distract me from the gas pain in my stomach.

I fall asleep for another little while, and when I wake up, Dr. Maltz is talking to my mom.

"Hey, Al," she says, smiling really big. "How are you feeling?"

"Okay, I guess." *Ready to be cured*, I think. *Just tell me what I have to do to make my stomach stop hurting.*

"I was just saying how well you did, but I was also telling your mom that there definitely is inflammation, and you have a number of ulcers in your lower colon and rectum." She holds out a piece of paper. "Those are some of the pictures we took."

"Some inflammation?" I ask. "Is that bad? Can I see?"

Dr. Maltz nods and adjusts it so I can get a better look. There are a bunch of circles showing something soft and pink and puffy. "Those are photos of your intestines," she tells me. "And you can see here"—she points to a picture in the center where everything is red and swollen—"that you have a lot of inflammation. That's a pretty clear sign of disease. I don't want to say anything firmly yet, though. I need to see what the biopsy looks like before making a diagnosis."

A pretty clear sign of disease.

That's what she said.

A pretty clear sign that I'm sick. That there's something wrong that's bigger than just a couple of incidents.

Even though there's no food in me, my intestines squirm at this news.

"Is that bad?" I ask again, more frantic this time.

Dr. Maltz smiles. "It just means we have to have a conversation about a diagnosis and a treatment plan."

"But it can be cured, right?" I ask. "Like, you can fix it."

"Let's talk about it at your follow-up appointment, okay?" Dr. Maltz says. "I'll give you all the information you need then, but for the time being I have to wait for the lab results to confirm some of my suspicions."

She tells my mom to schedule a follow-up appointment to go over my diagnosis, but I'm hardly listening.

I'm sick. There's disease. Dr. Maltz keeps talking and smiling as if this is just a normal day for her, and maybe it is. She's probably about to go walk over to the kid in the next hospital bed and change their life forever too.

"We'll talk soon," Dr. Maltz says, and I tune back into the conversation. "For now, get some rest. I'm sure this has been a tough day for you."

I nod, though "tough day" feels like an understatement.

We just learned about the eruption of Mount Vesuvius in my social studies class. The volcano exploded and then all the residents of the ancient city of Pompeii were covered in ash and debris.

If this was a "tough day" for me, then that was a "tough day" for the people of Pompeii.

"SURPRISE!" Leo shouts when my mom opens the door to our apartment.

"Let her rest, bubs," Beth says, grabbing Leo's shoulders. But she's smiling. "Welcome home, Al."

I smile back at them. It's nice to come home to Beth and Leo, especially after a day like today. Even with Leo wanting to do drama club and be more involved at school (gross), he and his mom are still the people who make me feel the most at home of anyone in the world.

There's a large sign hanging up above the couch that says IT'S A COLONOSCOPY! It clearly used to say IT'S A BOY! but Leo crossed out BOY and wrote COLONOSCOPY. Normally I would think that's super funny, but right now I just need to lie down.

My mom walks me over to the couch, and I don't fight it. I flop onto my stomach to try to relieve the pain. Dr. Maltz warned me that I might have a lot of gas pains, because they pump your intestines full of air during the procedure, and this is the only comfy position right now.

"How was it?" Leo asks, sitting down next to me. "Did it hurt?"

"Not really," I tell him. "I don't even remember it."

My mom's whispering something to Beth, probably telling her that the colonoscopy gave us all definitive proof that I'm defective and that I'll never have a normal poop again, like the ones I used to have in the good old days. When my mom finishes whispering, Beth reaches out to rub her shoulder, which is nice of her. My mom seems extra stressed out lately—obviously because of me. But at least she has Beth.

"I bookmarked a bunch of TikToks for us to watch when you were done with the colonoscopy," Leo says as he pulls out his phone.

I grin and scootch over so he can lie down next to me. "That's the best thing you could possibly say."

We're on our stomachs, squished together on the couch. The TikToks are a mix of things: One's about a dog who lives near the North Pole getting a bath, another is a video of one of the *HSMTMTS* actors playing a song on her ukulele. All of them are perfect, because Leo picked them out for us to watch together.

After a few minutes of this, Beth asks if we're hungry.

"A little," I tell her, adjusting the pillow on the couch and bringing my legs into my chest.

"Great," she says. "I made challah French toast!"

I might be gassy and tired and incurably poopy, but all I want in the world is some of Beth's challah French toast. My mom used to make it for me with store-bought challah on Saturday mornings, back before she read every blog about foods that are "easy on the stomach." But Beth's challah French toast is oily on the outside and fluffy on the inside, and it's all made by hand, for us. Well, really it's for the customers at the bakery, but still. If Beth's challah is my favorite bread, her challah French toast is my favorite thing to eat, period.

"I can even bring a tray over and you can eat it on the couch," my mom says, rubbing my hair back.

I don't know why she's letting me have something so "hard on my stomach," but maybe it's like a last meal. This might be the only time she'll let me have something this delicious until I, like, leave for college. And even then she'll still text me things like "I checked the menu of the dining hall and the best thing for you is bran flakes!"

Or maybe that won't be my life, because there's still a chance that whatever Dr. Maltz is going to diagnose me with will go away and these first few weeks of seventh grade will feel like a bad, poop-filled dream.

I nod to my mom that I'd like my food on the couch, and everyone bustles around me. It's weird being doted on like this. I don't like feeling like I'm incapable of doing something for myself, but in this case I really can't.

Plus, I love that my mom and Beth are better friends now, because it means that the four of us can be here in this apartment with freshly made challah French toast and maple syrup and tea and coffee. The smells waft over from the kitchen, mixing like the best scented candle in the world.

Leo plops down on the floor by the couch to eat, and my mom and Beth sit nearby at the kitchen table, chatting quietly. The French toast is warm and sweet and delicious, and I eat it as slowly as possible. I don't want to upset my stomach even more after the day it's had.

When we've both finished, Leo and I watch some more TikToks on his phone while my mom and Beth keep laughing and eating and chatting nearby. All in all, it's pretty nice. It feels right.

Like home.

And somehow, I'm not *quite* as worried about my stomach now that it's filled with a meal that Beth made. The disease, whatever it is, can't be so bad if it can handle all of that.

A few minutes later, I fall asleep to the sound of Beth's and my mom's laughter, Leo sitting by my side.

Chapter Eight

NO MORE MR. NICE BODY

It's time. After a few days of waiting, I'm back at the hospital, ready for Dr. Maltz to seal my fate with a diagnosis.

I saw someone on TikTok say that there was going to be a big shooting star and that we should all make a wish. I dragged Leo outside with me, who dragged Beth, who dragged my mom. I didn't think she would want to come, but she squeezed my hand as the star crossed the sky.

I focused all my energy on wishing, hoping, praying. Whispering to myself, "There will be a cure, things will go back to normal," over and over.

Now that I'm at the appointment, I repeat the words again, only this time it feels less like a wish and more like a lie I'm telling myself.

When Dr. Maltz walks into the room at the follow-up appointment, I hold my breath, as if that'll stop her from saying whatever it is she's about to tell me.

She sits down and leans forward in her seat. "Well, Al, the tests confirmed that it's definitely Crohn's."

My mom furrows her brow and asks what that means. She wants more information.

I don't want more information, though. Because if I ask for it, Dr. Maltz might tell me the exact thing I don't want to hear: That there's nothing she can do to make my bathroom emergencies stop. That I'm going to be running to the porta potty in the afterlife (if there is one).

"I'm going to give you two some pamphlets to read at home," Dr. Maltz says. "But the gist of it is that Crohn's is a chronic inflammatory condition of the gastrointestinal tract." Dr. Maltz looks over at me. "Do you know what *chronic* means?"

"Um, kind of? Like, basically." I stare at the examination table. "But can you say it too so I know for sure?"

"Of course," Dr. Maltz tells me. "I love it when my patients want to learn and advocate for themselves and their health."

She grins and I give her a closemouthed smile back. I don't want to *learn* or *advocate*. I want to be *normal*. For her to tell me that Crohn's is something that can go away with a bit of medicine.

Dr. Maltz takes a breath. "So, a chronic condition means it's going to be something you have to manage long-term, and it doesn't have a cure. There will be times when it's better and times when it's worse, but it'll never go away completely."

I sit there for a moment, trying to process what she said.

Because it sounded a lot like *It doesn't have a cure.*

Crohn's disease, the disease I now have—or have maybe always had—is what's causing my bathroom emergencies. And it will never go away. I'm always going to be sick. I'm never going to go back to how things were before, when my stomach worked like it was supposed to.

I can see out of the corner of my eyes that my mom's looking at me, but I keep staring at the cold metal table.

So much for the shooting star.

Dr. Maltz continues, "With medication, hopefully we can manage your pain and get you feeling better and living a fairly normal life. Some people go into remission for years, which means that their symptoms are gone for a while." She smiles at me. "Do you have any questions?"

I shake my head. Even if medication *can* help, it won't solve anything. This can't be fixed, it can only be *managed.* I don't want to be managed. I want to be *normal.*

"So is Crohn's what's causing the ulcers and inflammation?" my mom asks, her voice quieter than usual.

"It is," Dr. Maltz says. "Crohn's is an auto-immune disease, which means that it causes your immune system to fight against you, even though its job is to protect you. So, your immune system attacks your gastrointestinal tract, and *that's* what's giving you all that inflammation and the ulcers."

I nod this time, but I don't understand how I'm supposed to keep all this information in my head. Dr. Maltz is telling me that my body is attacking itself. My body that has already caused me so much pain and embarrassment. The one that's never going to be normal.

I wish I could just start over, respawn into a healthy body like a video game character.

Dr. Maltz talks for a while. She pauses to ask if my mom and me have any questions, but we keep shaking our heads. Finally, she tells me she's going to start me up on some medicine called mesalamine, which is going to make my immune system stop attacking my gut, but it'll also make me weaker since I won't be able to fight off infections as well.

Super cool. Not only am I sick, I also might get *more sick* just from the medicine I have to take that's supposed to make me better.

I'm ready to bolt from the hospital, when Dr. Maltz says, "Have you given any thought to the IBD support group?"

I shake my head, even though I *have* given thought to it, and the thought is, *Please, no.*

"I really think it might be good for you," Dr. Maltz says.

"I agree," my mom adds, which makes the idea of the group about a thousand times worse.

Dr. Maltz smiles at me. "You shouldn't have to hold all of this in."

"Maybe," I tell her. *When pigs fly and I never have to poop again.*

Chapter Nine

I'M NOT CRYING IN THE SPECIAL BATHROOM, YOU ARE

The first day of having a chronic—aka incurable, aka will be with me forever, aka my new best friend is an inflamed colon—illness at school has been pretty much the same as every other day. I've pooped a couple of times (bloody, of course, because it's not like my medicine's gonna work after a day), and I've tried my best to hide every part of my body, wearing even baggier clothes than usual so that people forget I have skin and organs underneath the fabric.

The only difference is that now I know that nothing I do matters, because I'll have Crohn's until I die, probably of embarrassment. I just want to go home, but of course, I can't. Because I promised Leo I'd walk with him to his audition after school.

"You can't say good luck, okay?" Leo says. He looks like he just saw a ghost in the hallway. "You have to say break a leg. You *have* to."

He's more nervous than I've ever seen him. Maybe that means he'll flub his audition and our Al and Leo Club can go back to normal.

"Break a leg," I tell him firmly, shaking the thoughts out of my head. Because I believe in him, and I don't want him to be stressed.

"But what if I actually break my leg now?"

Leo starts to hyperventilate, and I put a hand on his shoulder. "You're not going to break your real leg."

He runs over to the side of the hallway and knocks on a wooden door. "You have to knock on wood too. Or your head."

I knock on my head. When Leo gets like this, all nervous and superstitious, you just have to do what he says. It would be mean not to.

We spent hours last night going over his audition song. I played the ukulele and he sang, swinging his arms and jumping around the room.

I told him he was incredible, that everyone at auditions would love him. Which was true, even if I didn't want it to be. The whole time he was rehearsing, I was thinking about what I'm supposed to do while he's at drama club. Why did he have to choose this year of all years to join a club, when my body's failing and the kids we've known forever are starting to smell weird and kiss each other? I just need one thing to stay the same—one thing!

When we reach the auditorium, a tall kid wearing all-black clothes hands us both a piece of paper. "Fill it out with your name, vocal range, and audition song, then give it back to me," they say, before turning to another group.

"Uh, I'm not auditioning," I try to tell them, but it's useless.

"That's the stage manager," Leo whispers. "You just have to do what they say."

I raise my eyebrows at him. The stage manager is kind of intimidating, but anyone who has that much control over a group of middle schoolers is cool in my book.

I recycle my piece of paper as discreetly as I can. It doesn't matter how powerful this person is—there's no way they're getting me to perform in front of people. Leo just stares at his audition form.

"Ecretsay andshakehay?" I ask him.

He nods, and we do our "in public" silent handshake (though we whisper "Mateys for life" for good luck, because, duh), then he takes a deep breath and walks into the auditorium.

I take a deep breath too and make a beeline for the special dressing room bathrooms that are only open when drama club is meeting or auditions are being held. The gurgling feeling in my stomach has been building up since the final bell rang.

There's no one in here, so I lay down some toilet paper, take a deep breath, and cry.

Leo's not mine anymore. The moment he walked into the auditorium, I could feel the Al and Leo Club dissolving. He stepped into a world that doesn't include me.

Now I'm just the Al Club, which is the worst group in

existence because I'm just one sick kid whose entire wardrobe is made up of oversized T-shirts and whose backup TikTok is full of girls kissing.

And if Leo gets cast in the show, I really won't have *anyone*.

How am I supposed to find someone who understands any of that?

I don't even scroll through my For You page. I just sit on the toilet and cry.

When I'm pretty sure that Leo has finished his audition, I pull the neckline of my sweater up to my face to rub away the last few tears dripping down my cheeks and make my way back to the stage doors. Leo's waiting for me.

"I think it went really well," he says, grinning.

I can't say the same.

Chapter Ten

ONE BITE OF CAKE IN EXCHANGE FOR MY SOUL

So, Leo got the role he wanted in the show.

It's only been a couple of days since the auditions, but, according to Leo, the director likes to put out the cast list as soon as possible.

We're about to have a celebration for Leo at his apartment, but my stomach's so bad that I can't get off the toilet.

I watch some TikToks that my mutuals on my backup account posted. Most of them are other queer middle schoolers, though none go to my school. I bet they'd unfollow me if they knew I was watching their TikToks on the toilet.

They don't even know what I look like. I have a Picrew as my profile picture, and I never, ever post videos. I want my mutuals to know more about me, but I'd never show my face on my backup. Then they'd know I'm a real person and not a pixelated drawing.

"Al," my mom calls out. "Finish up, Leo's almost home!"

And that's the final straw. My mom babies me half the

time, making sure I have applesauce and that I get to bed at an appropriate hour, but now she wants me to just get off the toilet when it's convenient for her.

I dig my fingers into my thighs and roll my eyes so hard that they hurt when they're back to their normal position.

I don't even have to poop anymore, but I stay on the toilet for ten more minutes, out of spite.

"SURPRISE!" my mom and Beth shout as Leo walks into our apartment.

He covers his mouth with his hands. "Is this for me?"

I'm standing in the corner, arms crossed. Leo looks over at me expectantly, and I point to the sign, smiling a little. "Um, obviously."

He immediately runs over and gives me a hug.

The sign says IT'S A LEAD! It was my turn to buy a poster from the drugstore that said IT'S A GIRL and cross out the word GIRL so I could write LEAD.

Because that's what Leo is now: a lead in the show.

He got cast as Rooster in *Annie Jr.*, who's Miss Hannigan's brother. It's a *really* big part. At least for a seventh grader who's never done theater before.

"I'm so proud of you, bubs," Beth says, handing Leo a bouquet of flowers.

"Aren't you supposed to give these to me on opening night?"

"Why not both?" she asks, then looks over at my mom and smiles. "We're celebrating."

Beth opens up a sparkling apple juice and cuts into half of a day-old dark chocolate cake from the bakery. My mom grabs utensils, and they slice and plate like a well-oiled machine.

I manage to swallow a bite of cake, but I know if I eat more than that it'll make me nauseous. My stomach doesn't hurt that badly, but I'm just not in the mood to eat at a time like this.

"Rooster is a great role," my mom says to Leo between bites of cake. "That must be a big time commitment."

It feels like she's rubbing it in my face.

"It is! The leads have rehearsals four days a week," he says excitedly between sips of apple juice. "Because we have to do blocking and choreography and music practice. And they said it doesn't even matter that I don't read music because I was able to copy the notes they played on the piano and apparently that's good enough."

"That's amazing," my mom says, grinning at him.

There's a pang of jealousy in my stomach that I try to tamp down. It's hard to see my mom look at another kid like that, with pride instead of worry. But then Leo's words sink in.

"Wait, four days a week?" I ask, and Leo nods. "So, I'm basically never going to see you again?"

"I'll be a little busier, I guess," he says. "But we'll still hang out on the weekends and stuff. I just have to make this a priority. I signed a contract and everything, saying that the only thing more important than the show was homework or if I have a family emergency."

I nod, but only so that no one notices that I'm blinking back tears.

I really am never going to see him again, especially since he's with his dad every other weekend.

"Maybe Al can work on the show too!" my mom says. "As long as her doctor approves it!"

I stare down at my lap, and while I'm looking anywhere but my mom's face, I see her reach for Beth's hand under the table and give it a squeeze. It's like they're better friends than me and Leo now.

"Yeah, you could do stage crew!" Leo chimes in after a second. I snap my head up. "Then both of our names could be in the playbill!"

"I did stage crew back in high school," my mom says, smiling and pulling out her phone. "One of my friends *just* posted a great photo of all of us on Facebook from back in the day. Let me pull it up." She uses her index finger to navigate her phone, then taps on something and turns it around to show us.

Beth leans in close to see the photo, then takes the phone from my mom's hands, showing it to me. "You and your mom could practically be twins from this picture."

I reluctantly look at my mom's phone, and Beth is right. It's like I'm a clone of my mom, even though we're entirely different people. It's the first thing people see when they look at us, that we have the same eyes and nose and mouth and hair and all of that superficial stuff.

Beth tries to show Leo the picture too, but he's glancing down at his hands. "Cool," he says in a way that makes it clear he doesn't think it's cool. At least we agree on that.

"But maybe you can ask the director if you can do something a bit more relaxed, like designing posters?" my mom suggests after Beth hands her phone back. "I'm sure Dr. Maltz would be okay with that."

"Mom, stop," I say quietly.

I wrap my arms tightly around my middle. I don't want her talking about my body and what it can or can't do. It's like she thinks I became a different person when my stomach started hurting. Someone who can't even stand up to paint sets or whatever it is people on stage crew do.

Plus, I'd never do stage crew in the first place. It's so frustrating. Why would I want to do something where I would have to sit back and watch Leo make friends who aren't me?

"I think I'm probably too busy for that," I tell them all, teeth clenched.

"What are you doing besides hanging out with me?" Leo doesn't say it in a mean way, but it still hurts my feelings. Even if I don't have other things to do, I still have a life.

Kind of.

Um, I'll be scrolling through TikTok and hiding from the world in my room and pooping (though hopefully less).

But then I remember that there *is* something I could do after school during the weeks while Leo's at rehearsal.

"I have the IBD support group," I tell everyone.

My mom raises her eyebrows at me. "You do?"

"You didn't tell me there was a group," Leo says at the same time.

I shrug.

If I go to the support group, I'll get them all off of my back, like the poop that escaped my underwear when I had my accident in gym. (Maybe things are worse than I thought).

"Yeah, I just think I want to be around other kids like me."

I don't know if that's actually what I want, because the idea of talking to other kids from school about poop is terrible, but at least it's something that I can do without Leo.

"Oh," Leo says, looking down at his crocs. "I guess that makes sense."

"It does," I say, more for myself than him.

Maybe if I go, it'll make up for all our time apart. *Maybe*.

"I'm doing it," I say finally.

So, it's settled. I'm going to go to sick kid support group because my best friend's abandoning me and I don't want to be stuck at home with my mom.

This should be fun.

Chapter Eleven

EMUS AND KOALAS AND CAPYBARAS, OH MY

My mom acts like I just told her I won the Nobel Peace Prize when I ask her to drive me to the support group.

"I can even go in with you!" she says as she grabs her keys. "I can introduce myself and make sure they know that you just got diagnosed!"

I would rather poop on the hospital floor, I think. "I'll be fine."

I honestly wish I'd never agreed to go to this group, but Leo's been at rehearsal or talking about rehearsal or dreaming about rehearsal every hour of every day, and I don't really have anything else to do. I got so bored after school today that I read the pamphlet Dr. Maltz gave me. I didn't learn anything about Crohn's except that the people who write pamphlets about it think kids still say "golly!"

But when my mom drives off and I walk through the hospital lobby, I realize that I didn't think this through.

I don't want to talk about poop with people from school. All I really want to do is sit at home with Leo and watch

TV and then go to bed at a reasonable hour and do it all over again, every day.

But Leo isn't home. He's at rehearsal. And I need to do something with all the free time I have now.

Alternatively, I could hide in the bathroom until my mom comes to pick me up. No one would even question it. I could say I was pooping.

"Hi!"

I jump a little. The person who popped out of nowhere to greet me is tall with shoulder-length black hair and a giant smile.

"Are you here for the support group?" she asks.

I nod. There goes my hide-in-the-bathroom plan.

"Great! I'm Dr. Alvarez, but you can call me Aneliza." She smiles brightly at me.

"Are you a gastroenterologist?"

She laughs. "No, I'm not *that* kind of doctor. I'm a social worker, which means I help kids and their families when they're going through a hard time." She steps aside so that the path to the door is open. "Wanna come in? We have vegan and gluten-free cookies! And the regular ones too, if that's more your style."

I nod and follow Aneliza into the room, standing a few feet behind her so that the other kids don't notice me.

But it's too late for that. A short kid with bright blue eyes and floppy brown hair partially hidden under the hood of a giant sweatshirt points at me and says, "New kid! Woo!"

Great, thanks for that, I think. He looks like someone the Addisons would have a crush on, which doesn't help.

Aneliza moves over so that everyone can get a good look at me, and I feel like a freak even though I know that all of these kids also have IBD.

I'm an outcast in a group of outcasts.

I feel like a zoo animal on display until a girl with curly brown hair wearing a choker with tiny hearts walks right up to me and says, "I'm Mina, and that's Ethan." She points to the kid who just shouted at me. "He's excited 'cause we haven't gotten a new person in like a year."

"What, you're bored of me already?" This comes from a lanky kid wearing a Mets shirt whose hair is in long twists. I vaguely recognize him from school, which confirms my worst fears: Kids who walk the same halls as me are gonna hear about my poop. Well, if I ever talk.

"We were bored of you when you first got here, Carl," Mina says, and everyone laughs—including Carl.

There are only four other kids here besides me, and they all seem to know each other really well. They have inside jokes and I have stomach cramps.

I hadn't gotten a good look at the fourth kid, but now that I do, I recognize them from Leo's audition.

I must stare at them for a second too long, because they say, "You were at drama club, weren't you?"

"Um, no," I say quietly. "I was just dropping my friend off."

"Wait, yeah!" They're excited now. "I handed you an audition sheet! How come you didn't audition?"

Because I'd rather use a porta potty with no soap every day for the rest of my life than perform in front of people from school.

I land on, "Just didn't really want to," then ask, "How come you're not at rehearsal?"

"I leave a bit early on support group days."

Aneliza smiles between the two of us, but the stage manager doesn't say anything else. I only recognize them and Carl from school, though, so that's good.

Then Aneliza moves to sit down in one of the chairs in the circle, and Mina follows her, so I do the same.

Aneliza smiles around the circle. "How about we do introductions?" she asks once everyone's settled down. "We can all say our name, what grade we're in, our pronouns if you'd like, if you have Crohn's, ulcerative colitis, or both, and our favorite animal. I'll go first. I'm Aneliza, I haven't been in middle school for a long time but technically I'm in twentieth grade because I just finished four years of graduate school, my pronouns are *she/her*, and my favorite animal is a toucan."

Everyone laughs at the twentieth grade part.

The kid from my school in the Mets shirt—Carl—goes next. "I'm Carl, I'm in seventh grade, my pronouns are *he/him*, I have ulcerative colitis, and my favorite animal is a tie between a shark and a T. rex."

"Um, no it's not," Mina says. "You have, like, a thousand pictures of koalas saved on your phone."

Carl puts his head into his hands, but I can tell he's smiling. "Fine, whatever, yeah. I like koalas. But I also like sharks." He turns to me. "*Jaws* is one of my favorite movies."

"I don't even get how liking koalas is embarrassing," Mina says. "Are boys not supposed to like cute animals? That's complete crap. Just because you're a boy doesn't mean you have to only like sharks and T. rexes."

"I know that," Carl says. "Let's try this again: My favorite animals are sharks, T. rexes, and koalas. Are you happy?"

Mina smiles at him. "Very. I'm next. I'm Mina, obviously. I'm in seventh grade, my pronouns are *she/her*, I'm a Crohn's disease girlie, and my favorite animal is a capybara because they're the largest rodents in the world." She smiles over at me, and I smile back. After a few seconds of that she says, "Um, it's your turn."

I almost run out of the room right then and there, because I thought she was just smiling *at me*.

Being a human being who has to speak and poop and eat and exist is the most mortifying thing in the world. I wish I could be one of the animals that people have mentioned instead.

"Sure, yeah. I'm Alison, but I go by Al, I'm in seventh grade, my pronouns are *she/her*, I guess"—I mean, *she/her* is close enough—"and my favorite animal would probably have to be . . ." I try to think of a single animal that I like. I don't want to say something too simple, especially after Mina said a capybara. Then I remember this TikTok I saw about an emu named Karen who's really rude to the people who take care of her. I like Karen. "My favorite animal is an emu," I say definitively. "Oh! And I guess I have Crohn's? Not ulcerative colitis." I feel so out of the loop. I'm not even sure what the difference is, to be honest.

Mina nods in approval. "I would've picked an ostrich over an emu, since ostriches are actually the tallest birds, but emus are good too."

"Remember what I said last time about active listening, Mina?" Aneliza asks.

"I'm actively listening," Mina tells her. "Isn't talking just the *most* active listening?"

The other kids laugh. Clearly this is how Mina usually is. Which is . . . loud, I guess.

"I'm Rikako," the stage manager says, starting the introductions back up again. They have their nails painted a mix of blue and green and have perfectly winged eyeliner. I could never wear something that bold, something that drew so much attention to myself. They remind me of some of the cool people I watch on TikTok, ones I know I could never be friends with in real life. Or thought I couldn't, at least. "I'm in eighth grade, *they/she*, Crohn's, and my favorite animal is an Old English sheepdog, because they're cute and they're good at herding, just like me with the actors in my shows."

I perk up at the *they/she* part. I want to talk to them

about that, but I don't think I have the guts to bring it up (though I have the guts to poop my brains out). Anyway, it's enough to have to sit through an hour of poop talk. No way am I going to mention who I like or my thoughts about my gender.

But regardless of all of that, it's really exciting that there's an eighth grader in the group. Right now I'm not friends with anyone whose name doesn't rhyme with Shmeo, but being friends with an eighth grader? That's next level. Or at the very least, we'll be in the same support group.

Well, if I come back.

"All right, one more introduction and then we can get started," Aneliza says, gesturing toward the kid in the big sweatshirt. "Go ahead."

"Uh, yeah, I'm Ethan, seventh grade, *he/him*, UC, emperor penguin for sure." Ethan lifts his chin to nod at me.

"Great!" Aneliza claps her hands together. "So, now that we all know a bit about each other, I thought I'd tell Al what this group is all about, and remind everyone else about some of the expectations." Mina pulls one of her legs up onto the chair and flops over her knee dramatically. "Everything you say here stays here. You can complain about your doctors, about your disease, about your friends and siblings, even about your parents, but the one thing you can't do is be disrespectful to each other." Aneliza smiles at me. "It's okay if you don't have anything to say today, Al. You can just listen to everyone else. And if you have a lot to say, that's great too!"

There's no way I'm gonna have anything to say. I've spent the past few weeks avoiding poop talk like the plague (or like the porta potty), and now suddenly I'm just supposed to know exactly how to talk about my own feces. No way. Nuh-uh.

But I do kind of want to hear what other people have to say.

"Can I start?" Rikako asks, and Aneliza nods. "My poop was really bloody this week, which sucks because I honestly thought my new meds were kicking in."

They go on to talk about her brother getting into college and how stressed their parents have been, and no one bats an eye at her saying something about bloody poop. This is the first time I've ever heard someone talk about what goes on in the bathroom like it's normal. Like having bloody poop is something everyone goes through—which I guess here it is.

I still don't want to talk, but I sit up straighter in my seat. Ethan goes next, telling us about how last weekend he went to his cousin's house with Rikako and they all had to share one bathroom. As he talks, Mina leans over to whisper to me. "Ethan and Rikako are dating and Ethan never shuts up about it."

"They are?" It's out of my mouth before I can stop myself.

I can't imagine dating anyone while having Crohn's; it would be mortifying. But maybe since they both have it, there's nothing to be embarrassed about.

"Yeah," Mina whispers. "They're kind of cute, honestly."

"Let's keep the conversation for everyone," Aneliza says pointedly to Mina.

I focus on Ethan, and now he's talking about how his best friend laughed when he farted, but then the fart turned out to be poop, and he had to hide in the bathroom and try to clean it up.

I've never had a poop emergency at Leo's apartment (I can just run back to my own bathroom), but it's wild that this happened to Ethan and he didn't eject himself into outer space.

"That's happened to me," Mina says. "I mean, before I had my bag."

I try not to laugh at the way Mina butts in on every conversation. It really is funny, though—she has so much to say, and she's not afraid to say it.

"Remember, Mina," Aneliza says, pointing to her ears. "Listening."

"Wait, what bag?" I ask.

"My colostomy bag," Mina says, lifting up her shirt a little to reveal a bag on her stomach covered in rainbow fabric. I stare at it, even though I know I shouldn't. "Have you never ever heard of one before?"

I shake my head, and try to stop the prickle of tears stinging the corners of my eyes. Even in a group of kids with the same disease as me, there's stuff I don't know. I thought just having IBD was enough to be here, but now I feel like there was required reading that I missed.

Aneliza smiles at me gently. "This is a great place to learn and ask questions," she says. "You just got your diagnosis, which can be a really scary time. Maybe Mina can tell you a little bit about her colostomy bag after Ethan's done with his story?"

I nod, and Ethan finishes talking about his accident at his friend's house, which makes me want to give him a hug (if I were a hugger) and also scream "YES! THIS IS WHAT IT'S LIKE!"

"Okay, so back to *me*," Mina says loudly when he's done, and the other kids in the group laugh or shake their heads.

"So usually, I just tell people that it's because a bear attacked me and left a hole in my stomach, but since you also have Crohn's, I'll tell you the whole story." She sits cross-legged on her chair and leans forward. "Basically, there's an opening in my body that connects my intestines to the outside, and then my poop gets collected in the bag here." She lifts up her shirt again just a tiny bit and points to the bag. I want to look away, because it feels wrong to stare at her stomach, but she doesn't seem embarrassed. "I had surgery to remove part of my colon because it wasn't working right, and now I have this. That's basically it."

Aneliza smiles at her. "Thanks for that explanation, Mina. Do you mind if Al asks questions?"

Mina shakes her head and shrugs. "Nope," she says. "I'm an open book."

"That's okay," I say quietly, even though I have a ton of questions about Mina's colostomy bag. I sit back as the group moves on and everyone else shares.

The meeting ends pretty soon after that, though, and Aneliza sends us out into the lobby with leftover cookies to wait for pickup.

It wasn't as bad as I thought it might be. I could probably just sit and listen forever without adding anything of my own.

We all sit on these colorful chairs in the kids' lobby that look like dreidels. They're pointy at the bottom and they spin you around and there's enough for all of us.

"It's so cool that we have a new person," Mina says to the group as she spins in her red chair.

I'm starting to get a little nauseous from all the spinning, but I don't stop.

"Definitely," Rikako says, checking their phone as they spin, which is impressive.

"Should we add Al to the group chat?" Carl asks, balancing on the spinny chair on his knees.

I hold my breath at that. I'm worried someone will say no and then there will be this group chat that I know about but am not a part of.

I don't have to worry for long, because Mina hands me her phone and gets me to put my number in without any hesitation. "You obviously have to join." She adds me to the group chat and tells me that's where they talk about poop

and share IBD TikToks and talk about what they're reading and stuff like that. I hadn't even thought to search for
IBD TikToks yet, but I'm glad they exist.

"How was the meeting?" my mom asks when she picks
me up.

"Fine," I tell her, leaning against the window as I scroll
up through the group chat and watch the TikToks they've
sent.

"Was your stomach okay?"

"Fine," I say again. I'm over the questions about my
stomach.

When I get back home, I lie on my bed and watch more
IBD TikToks. I even learn the difference between Crohn's
and ulcerative colitis from one video, which is good
because I really didn't want to have to ask someone from
the support group. It's pretty simple actually, it's just that
ulcerative colitis can only occur in the colon, and Crohn's
can happen anywhere in your digestive tract, from your
mouth down to your butt. Because of course it can.

I don't know if I'll say much in the group chat, but I'm
glad I'm in it.

Mina's been writing in the chat the most. She even
sends a selfie with the caption "changing my bag 😊" and
everyone sends a poop emoji back.

It's so wild that the stuff I'm usually embarrassed

about—poop stuff—is completely normal to them. Or at least it seems that way.

And texting them feels different from texting Leo, but not in a bad way (just in a more poop-filled way).

The group chat is active into the night, way too late, long after I should be asleep. But I stay up, waiting for one more message, for one more poop emoji.

I fall asleep with the group chat open on my phone.

Chapter Twelve

SERGEANT ANCHOVY POOPS WITH HIS BROTHER

Our building is always weirdly quiet after Leo leaves for the weekend.

He was even more excited to leave than usual, because he's going to have a sleepover with his cousins on his dad's side. They live in Queens, and they have three elderly terrier mixes and an ice cream maker. But still, he could at least pretend to be sad to leave me.

I'm not jealous exactly, but whenever Leo comes home from a weekend with his cousins he always talks about all the food his tita makes and all the cool things they get to do. One time he even went to the New York Hall of Science without me, which was rude because he knows it's one of my favorite museums. I mean, they have a real-life rocket ship and a ropes course. A ROPES COURSE!

With Leo gone and having the time of his life without me, I have nothing to do but hang out in my room and poop and try to do my homework.

I try studying Spanish vocabulary, until I see that Mina started a FaceTime with the people from the support group. I guess that includes me now, and my stomach drops. I want to talk to all of them—especially Mina—but a group FaceTime is intense.

I take a deep breath, then press the notification and suddenly Mina's and Rikako's and Ethan's and Carl's faces are bouncing around in little squares on my screen.

"Al!" Mina says when I join.

"Um, hi," I say quietly. I'm worried that if I speak too loudly, they'll remember that they barely know me and kick me out.

"Wanna play Among Us?" Carl asks. He's lying down on his bed, a cat climbing over him in the background.

"Looks like Sergeant Anchovy wants to play too," Rikako says from their FaceTime square. I can see a glimpse of their bedroom behind them. It's bathed in a pink light and there are really cool neon signs of a mushroom and a sunflower in the background.

The cat—Sergeant Anchovy, I guess—meows.

"Wow that's sus," Ethan says, and we all laugh.

"Imposter for sure," Carl coos, petting Sergeant Anchovy.

"Anchovy has IBD too," Mina tells me.

Sergeant Anchovy passes in front of Carl's camera so that the only thing we can see is his butt.

"It's true," Carl says, moving Anchovy out of the way. "That's why I adopted him—I convinced my parents that we could help each other."

"Did it work?" I ask.

"Yeah," Carl says as Anchovy meows. "I mean, he always

sits on my lap when I poop—except if he needs to poop too."

Everyone cracks up at that, and I do too. All of our squares fill with laughter, and the anxiety I was feeling when I saw the notification on my screen fades to the back of my mind.

We play Among Us for a little while, which is this game where you're part of a crew on a spaceship and everyone has to do tasks, except that some people aren't *really* part of the crew—they're imposters there to sabotage you. Everyone in the group calls me the "silent killer" because I'm the imposter three times out of four and I don't talk at all but I win each time.

As I watch all the multicolored avatars of the kids from the support group run through the spaceship on my phone, I get a warm feeling in my chest all the way down to my toes. I imagine that we're all actually on the ship, in this bright place where we have tasks to accomplish and people to laugh and run around with.

"Al?" Beth calls from the hallway about an hour into the FaceTime. I have my bedroom door open since my mom's not home, so I hear her loud and clear.

I mute myself. "One second," I call to her. Then I unmute to tell everyone that I have to go.

"What? Why?" Mina asks.

"Just have to do something," I say, trying to hide the smile on my face.

It's nice to be wanted.

I put my phone under my pillow and open the front door.

"I just thought I'd stop by and bring you some dinner," Beth says, holding up a couple of Tupperware containers. "Since I know your mom's not going to be back from work for a while."

"Oh, cool." I grab the food. "Thanks."

Beth smiles. "Of course," she says, but she doesn't turn to leave. "Or . . . you could come across the hall and have dinner with me? Since we're both alone for the evening?"

We've never eaten dinner just the two of us—she's dropped off food for me when my mom's working late, or she'll have Leo bring something over, but never her and me alone.

"Uh, yeah, sure." I *do* want to have dinner with Beth. She makes the best food, and she's really funny.

So, I ignore how weird it is that Beth wants to have dinner just the two of us and follow her across the hall. While we're eating, we talk about Leo and school. I don't say too much, though, and she doesn't mind because I'm scarfing down dinner. She made egg and cheese sandwiches on homemade everything bagels that still taste fresh from the oven even though she probably baked them at, like, three in the morning, along with a "side" of honey chicken. Then Beth tells me about her plans for the bakery, how she might start a bread subscription service.

"That way people would never run out of challah," she says when she's done explaining the idea.

"You should definitely do that," I tell her as I lick a bit of sauce off my fork. "Are you gonna do any rainbow challah? I saw some at another bakery."

"Blech," Beth says, and she sounds so much like Leo, I almost turn to his bedroom to see if he's there, even though I know he's with his cousins. "Rainbow challah is for goyim," she says, and I giggle at that.

She's like the older version of Leo, sprinkling Yiddish words into conversation and making me laugh like only he can. It makes my heart hurt a little too, because she's not Leo, but right now she's the closest I'll get.

"Also, that chicken was *so* good," I say, changing the subject.

"That's your mom's favorite too," Beth says, smiling as she clears my empty plate that was once the huge "side" of honey chicken.

My eyebrows furrow as Beth turns to put the dishes in the sink. Honey chicken isn't my mom's favorite. It can't be, because my mom's favorite is . . . Well, okay, I'm not actually sure what my mom's favorite dinner is, but based on the amount of turkey sandwiches we eat, I assumed it was that.

"Cool," I say finally, hoping Beth doesn't notice how confused I look.

"How would you feel about honey apple cake?" she asks after a minute, rubbing her hands against her apron.

I smile, all the weirdness forgotten at the mention of cake.

"Really good," I tell her.

Beth's honey apple cake was one of the first things I ate from the bakery when we first moved into the apartment. It's fluffy and crumbly, and there are chopped-up walnuts and apples inside. She only makes it in the late summer/early fall around Rosh Hashanah, but with my poop problems I haven't had a single slice yet this year.

The cake smells amazing, but just as I take a giant bite, Beth asks, "So, how have your kishkes been?"

I want to glare at her, but I don't because it would be rude to glare at an adult who's not my mom.

"Fine," I tell her after I finish chewing and swallowing. "Much better, actually."

"That's great, bubs," she tells me, smiling like she genuinely means it. "Your mom told me that you went to your first support group meeting."

"Yup," I say, then chew awkwardly for a minute.

I wish she didn't have to know about me having Crohn's and everything that goes along with it, but maybe that's just part of the new thing she has going with my mom, where they text and talk all the time. I don't know how mom friends work.

"So, are you and my mom, like, best friends now?"

I'm only asking her because it really seems that way. And it's not like I'm complaining or anything—it would be awesome if my best friend's mom was best friends with my mom.

Beth looks down at her lap, then takes a bite of cake. When she's done chewing, she nods. "We're definitely closer." She takes a breath. "And since your mom and I *are* closer, I also wanted to let you know that you can always talk to me about anything, all right?" Beth reaches out her hand, but I don't know what to do, so I just flop mine down near hers. "You know that, right?"

I nod but don't say anything. We finish the apple honey cake in awkward silence after that.

"Thanks," I tell Beth, waving from the hallway between our apartments as I leave.

"You're so welcome, bubs." She smiles at me, sighs, and closes her door.

When I get back to my bedroom, I check my phone, and there are a bunch of messages from Mina.

Messages that are just to me, not the group chat.

MINA: im really glad u came to support group last week!
and that u hung out w us today!!!!
u should really keep coming

For the first time, the feeling in my stomach isn't a

brewing poop emergency. It's ... something else. Something fuzzier.

    ME: of course!!
    cant wait for next week!!!

And I really can't, not since we FaceTimed and played Among Us and joked together in our bedrooms.

Now that I don't have anything left to do for the day or anywhere to be, though, I go to the bathroom and sit on the toilet and scroll through my For You page some more. And even *that* feels different, because I know that I'm not the only one who spends whole nights on the toilet. Mina, Carl, Ethan, Rikako and I are all connected through our poop, as gross as that may be. We're probably even connected through the sewer system.

It all goes to the same place eventually.

Chapter Thirteen

CLINKING OUR APPLES TOGETHER

Leo has to go to the auditorium for extra rehearsal with a few other leads in the show, so I'm alone for lunch. It's been a couple of days, but I've barely seen Leo since he's been home from his dad weekend.

I slump down at a table in the far corner of the cafeteria and open up my bagged lunch—another day, another soggy turkey sandwich.

It's pretty quiet back here. The most popular people sit toward the entrance in the most visible spots, leaving the outer regions for everyone else.

"Hey, can I sit with you?"

I look up from my soggy sandwich to see Carl from the support group. He seems super nervous. His shoulders are hunched, and he took his twists out, so now his hair's in tight curls falling over his face.

"Yeah, sure." I move my math notebook off the seat next to me. I'm a little nervous too, honestly. The only thing I can think to talk about with him is having Crohn's, but that's not exactly lunchtime conversation.

We eat in silence for a while. At first, it's a little weird, but then it's kind of . . . peaceful. I like that he's down to just sit and eat quietly.

"How's Anchovy?" I ask after a few minutes.

"He's good, he's good." Carl takes a bite of his sandwich. "He had diarrhea last night. But so did I, so . . ." He shrugs like it's not a big deal that we're talking about poop at school. At *lunch*. When really this is the first time I've ever heard anyone talk like this at a meal. My mom will check on my stomach (of course), but she never speaks in specifics like this. My first instinct is to be grossed out, or to at least pretend to be, but I don't have to pretend. I can just sympathize. It's kind of great.

I don't know what to say, so we keep eating for a minute, until Carl takes a deep breath.

"I'm glad you're coming to support group now," he says quietly, staring down at his lunch. "Everyone thinks you're, like, really nice. And you're the only other seventh grader in the group who goes to school with me, so, yeah. I'm glad you're here."

I try not to grin too hard at that. "Yeah?"

He looks over at me and nods, but just for a second. "It's like in *Heathers* when JD comes to school and then Veronica finally has someone to hang out with."

"What?" I only understood like half the words in that sentence.

"It's an old movie," Carl explains. "And I guess it's not really like that because JD poisons someone, and I don't think you would do that."

"I wouldn't," I promise him, though that's probably obvious. Carl's the quietest one in the group, but he's cooler than I'll ever be.

"That's good," he says about me not poisoning people.

We both smile as we eat our lunches, letting the yelling and laughter from the rest of the cafeteria wash over us.

"OMG look at the two of you eating together!" I look up and see the stage manager—Rikako—walking up to our table. They pull up a chair from a half-empty neighboring table and slam their notebook down. It's massive and full of sticky notes and tabs. "First rehearsal on the real stage later," they tell me, pointing to the notebook. "I have to keep track of *everything.*"

"Cool," I tell her, though I don't know if it is. That notebook is the reason Leo's never home. Well, maybe the notebook itself isn't the reason, but I still stare at it like it is.

"Do you want an apple?" she asks Carl.

He nods and she hands it to him, then she looks over at me and pulls out a second apple.

"Want one too? I have extra." They toss it up into the air and catch it easily. "They're pretty easy on the stomach, for a fruit, so I like to carry them around."

Rikako grins at me, and I can't help but say "Sure," and she hands me a speckled red-and-yellow apple, then the three of us bite into them. I've never had an eighth grader offer me an apple, or say anything at all to me. I feel chosen and shiny, especially since she's the stage manager and the only interaction she has with Leo and the other drama kids is probably to yell at them.

But she's not yelling at me.

Rikako sticks their apple out toward the center of the table. "Cheers," they say. "To the newest member of our little club."

Carl grins, and I do too, and we both reach our apples out so they can all tap together.

"That's kind of nasty," Carl says.

"Yeah," I agree, laughing.

Rikako shakes her head and says, "I never said you *really* had to touch my apple," and Carl bursts out into giggles.

This is the first time in all of middle school that I've sat with someone other than Leo at lunch, and I don't want to go run and hide in the bathroom.

And if I did, they wouldn't even care.

"Can't you just skip today?" I whine as Leo and I walk over to the auditorium after the last bell rings that day.

It's not support group day, so I have nowhere to go and nothing to do without him. And I'm not about to reread the "So Your Butt Is Broken" pamphlet (that's not exactly what it's called, but still).

"No, I really can't," he says. "You can only be excused if you weren't in school today."

I'm trying to be supportive of Leo doing drama club (at

least to his face), but his performances have always been just for us and our moms, and now they're going to be for the whole middle school. It's like he's letting the whole world see a part of himself that, up until now, only I've been able to see.

Leo opens the auditorium doors and I follow behind him, not wanting the theater kids to see me and sense my distrust toward them and their jazz hands or whatever.

"Leo!" A tall pale kid with round glasses and round cheeks waves as he walks over to where Leo and I are standing. "I'm so excited for rehearsal today, oh my *god*. I'm still literally so glad you auditioned!" He says this excitedly, rocking back and forth on his heels.

"Yeah." Leo grins, but he's looking down at his shoes. "Me too."

"Well, it's perfect, because we needed more boys. Usually Liam Brambilla does it too, but this year he chose baseball over the show."

My stomach gurgles. I'm pretty sure it's the *this is awkward* gurgle. I can almost identify them now, like how parents know what their baby wants just from their cries.

"That sucks," Leo says.

The kid nods fervently. "It *does* suck."

"Peregrine, Ms. Bailey's saying we have to start now so people don't miss the late bus."

I look up at the person who said that, and it's a very familiar face. My stomach gurgles again, but this time it's the I'm-so-relieved-I-could-cry gurgle.

"Hey, Rikako!"

Her eyes widen and she grins at me. "Hey! Back for more, I see." She's holding a clipboard and wearing all black: black leggings, black Doc Martens, and a big black sweater.

"No, no," I say. "I was just dropping him off." I point to Leo, who smiles and waves.

"Well, if you ever wanted to do stage crew, we always need more hands."

I'm about to say no, *no way*, but Leo looks over at me, his eyes pleading. Plus, if Rikako's leading it, it can't be that bad. "I mean, like, maybe. If you *really* need help."

"Great! I'll add you to the list," Rikako says as they walk away purposefully, jotting my name on their clipboard as they do, sealing my fate.

"Well, I'm just glad you're here," Peregrine says. I don't think he's looked in my direction once during the whole conversation. "I wish Daddy Warbucks and Rooster had more scenes together."

Leo's face gets flushed and sweaty as he grins. "Yeah, same," he says.

"Rikako," Peregrine shouts as he walks away, loud enough for everyone in the auditorium to hear. "Can you call *five* for the actors?"

"Who was *that*?" I whisper to Leo after a few seconds.

"No one," he says. "Just the president of drama club."

"Oh." I kick at Leo's shoe so that he looks up at me. I don't know why this kid named after a falcon is making me super jealous, but he is. "Is he in eighth grade?"

"Yeah," he says. "But he's really down-to-earth. Like, he even talks to sixth graders."

"Rikako's in eighth grade too," I say. "They're in my . . . group thing."

"I guess we both know people in eighth grade now," Leo says, shrugging.

"Yeah." I tug on the loose sleeve of my sweater. "Wanna do homework together later?" I need him to say yes, to know that he still cares about our Al and Leo time.

"Actors, warmups starting in four minutes!" Rikako shouts from the front of the auditorium. "Phones off, jazz shoes on, let's go."

"That's my cue," Leo tells me, an apologetic look on his face. He waves goodbye, then runs over to a group of drama club people. He hops around as he tries to pull on his jazz shoes, laughing with the other kids in the show. They all flock around him—a few girls even pull him in for a selfie.

Maybe he didn't hear me when I asked about homework, or maybe he doesn't care. But it's weird to see him fit in so seamlessly here, when before he only fit with me. At least now I have the support group. He has his new friends, and I have mine.

Even so, it feels wrong to slip out of the auditorium doors and walk home, Leo-less.

Chapter Fourteen

THE BATHROOM CLUB

Here is the list of very impressive and important things I've accomplished while Leo's been at rehearsal: I've made and then unmade my bed so I could snuggle into the blankets, scrolled through a list of all the people the Addisons are following on Instagram, and wished for a time machine so that I could go back to before Leo ever auditioned for the show.

Today's Friday, and yet he *still* has rehearsal. What kind of club makes you meet on a Friday? If my mom and I observed Shabbos, I'd definitely complain. Leo and Beth will light candles, and the bakery is closed, but beyond that Leo will do homework and Beth will pay bills and stuff like that. Maybe I'll file a complaint anyway.

The whole apartment complex feels emptier without him. Knowing he was across the hall—even if he's not hanging out with me—would be a thousand times better than this.

Just as I'm about to move on to my next Leo-less activity

(maybe staring at the wall would be fun), I check my phone and see a message in the support-group group chat.

ETHAN: my mom just bought TONS of snacks from trader joes
hang at my place?

RIKAKO: uh yes obviously
did she get the chocolate-covered bananas

ETHAN: yea duh

CARL: what about the chili mangos tho

ETHAN: ur the only one who can eat those
they hurt my stomach so bad

CARL: guess that just means im too powerful

MINA: dude im in
and ur mom already knows the snacks i like

ETHAN: she knows the snacks **all** of you like
u ate a whole bag of the peanut butter pretzels last time

MINA: its not my fault that my BROTHERS ALLERGIC

i gotta stock up when i can
rude

RIKAKO: omg can u two calm down

MINA: no

ETHAN: nope

I smile down at my phone. I'm still shocked that they're including me in this group chat *and* inviting me to hang out.

I'm practically itching to go, but there's something—or someone—in my way.

My mom and Beth are hanging out just outside my door in the living room, watching some reality show about dog grooming. They're both laughing hysterically at all the poodles who are getting dyed pink and blue and green. "Hey, Allie," my mom says. She's clearly in a good mood, maybe from the show, or maybe from hanging out with Beth.

"Can I go to a friend's house?" I ask her.

She pauses the show, then turns to me, a concerned look on her face. "Which friend?"

"Just someone from the support group," I say. "His name is Ethan and as far as I know his parents aren't organ harvesters. Can I?"

Beth laughs at that, but my mom still looks worried.

"Are you sure that's a good idea?" she asks. "What if you have an . . . *emergency* in someone else's house?"

I cross my arms. "I'm not gonna have an *emergency*," I grumble. "And even if I did, everyone else there will have IBD, so they'd understand."

Unlike you, I think.

"It's a little late, Al," my mom says. "I have to be up early for work."

"I can pick her up," Beth chimes in. She's been watching the exchange this whole time, but now she's leaning forward, her leg brushing against my mom's. "I'm off tomorrow anyway."

"You don't have to do that, Bethie," my mom says.

Bethie? Since when does my mom call her *Bethie?*

I don't say that, though, because that would probably ruin my chances of going anywhere tonight, so all I say is, "That would be great!" and cross my fingers and toes, hoping that she agrees.

My mom turns to Beth, then sighs and gives in. "All right. When do you want to leave?"

I glance at my phone. "Now?"

Beth snorts, and my mom shakes her head and stands up to grab her keys.

I'm silent during the ride to Ethan's house, because it's all too good to be true.

"Text Beth when you're ready for a pickup, okay?" my mom asks. "And don't make her go out too late."

"I won't," I promise as I run out of the car.

There are pink flowers in every hue covering the path to the front door. My heart is racing and my stomach is clenched at the idea of knocking on the door, so I take a deep breath and text the group chat.

ME: im here!

MINA: we're in the basement!!
just walk around to the side door

I tiptoe around the house, hoping that Ethan's parents don't think I'm a burglar or something.

There's a door at the bottom of a small set of stairs, and there's music playing inside that sounds like it's from a video game.

I slip in quietly, and put my shoes next to the others in the entryway. The basement is completely wild. There's a Ping-Pong table in the center, a giant fridge, a couch across from a huge TV where Mina and Carl are playing Mario Kart, and a bunch of beanbag chairs lining the edges of the room.

"NO NO NO NO," Carl shouts, slumping back on the couch.

Mina grins and sticks her tongue out at him. "This just proves that Cat Peach is the best."

"No," Carl says again, shaking his head. "Bowser has the best stats."

They both see me and wave. "Al! You made it just in time

for the tournament." Mina jumps up from the couch and runs over to where I'm standing awkwardly by the door.

"You can't just beat us a million times and call it a tournament," Rikako says. She pushes herself out of the beanbag chair where she's been sitting with Ethan and wanders over toward the couch. Ethan follows them, so I go over there too so that the five of us are all slumped onto the enormous navy-blue sectional.

"Should we watch a movie or something?" Ethan asks.

Mina leans forward to grab a handful of chips from the pile of snacks on the coffee table.

"Ugh, no, that's so boring," she says at the same time as Carl says "Yes!"

"Since this is Al's first time hanging out with us, maybe she should decide what we do," Ethan suggests.

Everyone looks at me; it's way too much pressure.

Luckily, I don't have to come up with a response, because Carl jumps from his butt to his knees on the couch, looking excited. "Wait," he says, his eyes darting between all of us. "There are five people in our group now."

"So?" Mina asks.

"*So*, haven't any of you ever seen that old movie? *The Breakfast Club*?"

We all shake our heads. I think I've heard of it, but I haven't seen it.

"Well, it's about these five high schoolers who are in detention, and they don't know each other that well outside of that or anything. And they're all stuck there for the whole day and they become friends." This is the most I've heard Carl talk since I met him, except when he was talking about another old movie. It's cool that he knows so much about them.

"I still don't get what that has to do with us," Rikako says through a mouthful of chocolate-covered banana.

"Because we're like that, except that instead of detention, we're all connected because of Crohn's or ulcerative colitis or whatever."

"You said the movie's called *The Breakfast Club?*" Mina asks, looking just as excited as Carl, who nods. "Then we could be The Bathroom Club!"

We all laugh a little, but Rikako sits forward on the couch. "Wait, I *love* that," she says. "'The Bathroom Club.' It's perfect!"

"We should watch it!" Ethan says. "Then we can, like, tag ourselves, and say who's who."

"It's on Netflix," Carl adds, grinning. "So, it's easy to watch. It's a little inappropriate, though."

"I won't tell." Rikako glances around the room. "You know, as the eighth grader here."

"I won't tell either," Ethan says. "You in?" he asks Mina.

She rolls her eyes. "Fine, but only because I don't want to be one of the dud characters."

Ethan pulls Netflix up on the TV, and we all settle into the couch.

The movie is from the '80s, so it's all old and grainy.

But the girl who plays one of the main characters, Claire, is really cute, with wide pink lips and wispy red hair.

When I lean forward to grab some more snacks, I check to see if anyone else is as transfixed by her as I am. Rikako and Ethan are sitting shoulder to shoulder, and Carl looks like he's never been happier to do anything in his entire life than watch the movie. Mina's staring at Claire, but when the shot changes to show the whole group, she glances over at me, her eyebrows raised.

I want to keep watching her watch the movie, but instead I turn my gaze to the snacks.

"Mina, you're *totally* Bender," Ethan says through a mouthful of cheese puffs. "Since he's the leader."

"I would never rip out the pages of a book, though." Mina's eyes go wide. "That's, like, blasphemy."

We all agree that she's most like the bad boy, Bender, because he's loud and cool and causes chaos.

"Can we just watch the movie?" Carl asks.

"That's just what the nerdy guy would say," Rikako tells Carl.

"Yeah, that's totally you," Mina says.

"I'm not even gonna try to fight you on that." He shrugs. "I like that character the most anyway."

I'm about to say who I think Rikako is when she lets out the biggest fart I've ever heard in my life.

Everyone goes silent for a moment, the only sounds coming from the upbeat music on-screen.

And then Mina leans forward and nods toward Rikako. "That was your best one yet."

I look around, and no one seems fazed—Carl's eating chips, and Ethan's checking something on his phone.

My first instinct when I heard Rikako fart was to laugh, because that's what always happens. If someone farts in class, then people laugh, or the farter is some boy making a big deal of how gross he is.

But Rikako's fart just . . . happened.

It was magical.

After the next scene in the movie, I tell Rikako that they're definitely the character with wispy hair and bangs because she's really nice and can keep everyone in check.

"What about me?" Ethan asks.

"You're the jock," I tell him. I'm on a roll now. I didn't think I knew anyone well enough to assign them a character, but his and Rikako's are so clear. "Plus, your character is flirting with Rikako's character, and you two are dating."

"It's true," Ethan says, and he smiles so big at Rikako. It's really cute, but it also makes me a little sad because they get to have a relationship with someone who understands them and I don't know if I'll ever have that.

As I turn back to the movie, my stomach drops. There's only one character left and she's the loner girl who doesn't talk to anyone.

But before I can think about it too much, Mina points to

the screen and says, "That one's obviously Al, because she observes everyone and she knows what's going on." Then she adds quietly, "And she's really cute."

I freeze on the couch, trying not to combust from the heat in my face. When Mina smiles over at me, I smile back. I can't help it. Maybe she can see that my cheeks are red, but right now, I don't care.

She called me cute.

Or, well, the character.

About halfway through the movie, Ethan's mom comes downstairs. She's short and blond, and she smiles really big at all of us.

"Guess what?" she asks, grinning at Ethan, who grabs the remote and pauses the movie.

"Mom, no," he groans, anticipating what she's about to say. "We're not going outside."

"Well, for anyone who's *not* a Debbie Downer, there's a fire in the pit outside and everything you need to make s'mores!"

"YES!" Mina shouts, jumping up from the couch. "Thank you so much, Ms. Fienman."

"You're very welcome, Mina," Ethan's mom says.

"Al, you *have* to come see the fire pit." Mina runs to the other side of the room to grab her jacket. "It's so cool."

Ms. Fienman smiles at Mina. "I even put out the extra-dark chocolate just for you." Then she waves as she walks back upstairs.

Carl turns to face Mina. "If you go, you're gonna miss the end of the movie."

"You can tell us what happens," Mina says. She looks over at me, her loose curls bouncing around her shoulders. "Al, you coming?"

"Um . . ." Rikako and Ethan are doing their own thing, and Carl is super transfixed by the movie. *Someone* has to go with Mina. It might as well be me. "Sure, yeah."

So, Mina and I head out the basement door to the backyard. There's a huge patio, and Ethan's mom is standing by the bonfire, poking it with a stick.

"Girls!" she says excitedly when she sees us. "I'll leave you two to make your own s'mores, but I'll be right inside if you need anything, okay?"

"Thanks!" Mina says.

"Thank you," I tell Ms. Fienman, and she smiles at me before walking away.

"She's the best," Mina says when Ethan's mom is safely out of earshot, milling about their warmly lit kitchen. "She's kind of like a mom to me too, honestly. She sometimes even takes me to my appointments when my parents have to go to counseling."

"She seems really great," I tell her. I wonder if Ethan's mom is for her what Beth is for me.

"She is," Mina says, nodding.

I'm about to ask what Mina meant by "counseling," but then she grabs a stick, pushes a marshmallow into the end of it, and sets it on fire. I'm too shocked by the giant flames to speak.

"I like it to be burned," she says as flames engulf the innocent marshmallow.

After she blows out the fire it's completely charred, but she takes her index finger and thumb and pulls the crust off, crunching it in her mouth before sucking the inside of the marshmallow off of the stick.

"That's the best way to do it," she tells me while she pops another marshmallow over the fire.

"How come no one else wanted to come make s'mores?" I ask as I break off a piece of the chocolate bar (the best part of a s'more).

"I guess they just don't appreciate a good fire," Mina says, her marshmallow aflame again. She's smiling maniacally, her face lit up by the fire. Then she blows it out. "Just kidding," she says. "I don't really know. But I'm glad you're here."

I turn away when she says that. It's dark enough that hopefully she can't see my face blushing and my eyebrows knitting together from the pain in my stomach. It's not poop pain; it's something different, from the core of my body.

She sits cross-legged by the fire, and I sit next to her. Her face is glowing yellow, and I wonder if mine is too or if there's just something special about her—she looks beautiful.

I've never had a crush on someone in person before. Like, I've had crushes on girls on TikTok, but I've never liked someone I could talk to in person, someone who could show me how to roast marshmallows.

Someone who could like me back.

Not that Mina would like me back. She might not even like girls, which is fine. She can be a new friend, someone to talk to besides Leo.

Mina puts her hands out in front of the fire, like she's trying to warm them, even though it's not that cold out. "Did you know that there are these giant worms that live near hydrothermal vents at the bottom of the ocean?"

I raise my eyebrows. "What?"

She turns to me so that her knees are close to mine, and a bead of sweat drips down my armpit.

"There are some animals called extremophiles, which means they live in environments that would kill most living creatures." She reaches back to grab another marshmallow, squishing it between her fingers. "So, the worms live near vents that get up to, like, six hundred degrees. Which is hotter than this fire, basically."

I don't say anything, because I don't know what to say. And more than that, I don't want her to stop telling me about this thing she's clearly so excited about.

"And the vents come from undersea volcanoes, and they're so deep in the ocean that there's no sun and the pressure would crush a person's skull." She demonstrates by squishing the marshmallow between her fingers, then eating it. "Scientists didn't think that there could be any life down there, but they wanted to see the vents, so they went down on this submarine, and as it turned out there was a whole *ecosystem* at the bottom of the ocean."

I open my mouth like she just told me really juicy gossip. "Like, living things?"

She nods excitedly. "Yeah, and the main animals in the ecosystem are these six-foot-tall worms." She leans in closer, and I can barely breathe. "But wanna know the most amazing part?"

I nod, hanging on her every word.

"The worm is one of the only animals without any mouth or butt or guts. It doesn't even poop." She grins, and this time I'm the one who leans in closer.

"That's amazing," I say finally.

"I know," she says. "I didn't say that they were my favorite animal at support group, because they're really not, but they're the one I feel the most connected to." She lifts up her shirt a tiny bit to reveal the bottom of her colostomy bag, which is now covered in tie-dye washi tape. "They're like me—they don't have any guts, but they still survive. And they're even the basis of a whole ecosystem. One day I'm gonna be a nematologist. I'm gonna study worms in a lab and go down to the bottom of the ocean to see the tube worms in person."

"That's *amazing*."

She pulls her shirt back down, smiling to herself. I clear my throat.

"Can I ask about the . . ." I point to her stomach.

"My colostomy bag?" she asks, patting it gently through her shirt. "Yeah, of course."

"When did you get it?" I feel like I don't know anything about having IBD, but I want to know everything about Mina, and her IBD is part of her.

I guess that's true for me too, but when I think about my disease, it still seems scary and somehow separate from me. Mina's so open about her bag and stuff. She talks about it like it's as normal as her class schedule.

"Last year," she says. "It was tough when I found out I needed surgery, but I feel *so* much better now. I can eat way more food without getting sick." She takes a deep breath. "I think I just had to get over the fact that my body is completely different now. But in a good way."

I nod. "Oh, nice."

It's like she's bionic. She was in pain, and now she's not. I'm almost jealous.

"You know Klein's Bakery?" she asks. Before I can answer, she continues. "They have the *best* biscochos, and I can actually eat them now. My family used to get them every Shabbat." Her face falls. "My mom even used to say that they're better than the ones her grandma made."

"I actually live above the bakery," I say quietly once she's done.

I don't say that biscochos are one of Leo's favorites too. They're a Filipino dessert in addition to a Sephardic one, which is why Beth makes sure they're always on the menu.

"Wait, what?" she asks, grinning. "That's *so awesome*."

"Yeah." I grin back. "It is." Mina's gotta be the number one coolest person in the world, so for her to think something from my life is impressive is kind of incredible.

"Are you Jewish too?" she asks.

My mom always says that Jews love to know if other people are Jewish. It's, like, our favorite thing. I nod in answer.

"Which synagogue do you go to?" she asks. "I go to Shaare Zion, but it's mostly other Sephardic Jews, and I'm guessing you're Ashkenazi—just because a lot of people around here are, and I haven't seen you at my synagogue."

"No, yeah, I am," I say.

My mom and Beth are both Ashkenazi Jews. What that means is we're Jews who come from Eastern Europe.

"My dad's family is Ashkenazi, but we're not as close with them because they live in Connecticut. And my mom's family is from Syria, so she likes going to our synagogue since there are a ton of other Syrian Jews there." She bites her lip. "Or, like, she did. We haven't gone in a little while."

"Cool," I tell her. "I haven't been to synagogue in a really long time. Like, basically ever."

It's kind of embarrassing to admit, since I live above a

Jewish bakery and my best friend is preparing for his bar mitzvah and knows way more about Judaism than me.

"You can come with me sometime if you want," she says. "It's pretty fun."

"Um, maybe."

But I really can't think of anything scarier than going to synagogue with a girl who is cute and knows everything about giant tube worms and makes my armpits sweat and who I think I might have a crush on.

"Well, either way, you should definitely come hang at my place," she says as she stands from the fire pit.

She's being so casual, like she is about so many other things, that all I can do is nod. "Yeah," I say, staring up at her, watching the flames reflected in her eyes. I snap out of whatever trance Mina and the fire put me under. "Sounds good."

She reaches her hand out to me. "Should we go check on the others and brag about our s'mores?"

It's the first time I've ever held someone's hand who's not Leo or my mom. Not that we're really holding hands. Or whatever.

"Yeah, let's do it," I say, and I let her drag me back to the basement, her hand only leaving mine when we reach the door.

Chapter Fifteen

FARTS IN A BAG

"And this is Tarantula," Mina says, pointing to a giant spider in a glass tank in her living room. "Did you know that girl tarantulas can live up to thirty years? So, she's stuck with that name forever. Astor came up with it." She nods over to her younger brother, who's playing Fortnite on his Switch.

I'm at Mina's house the day after the eventful evening in Ethan's basement. She actually followed through on her invitation, and now we're "hanging." Just me and her.

Mina told me when we got here that her mom is home but that we shouldn't bother her because she's on a call, which is fine by me. I don't like talking to adults anyway.

After she gives me the tour of the first floor, Mina leads me up to her bedroom, which is in the attic. Her house is pretty small, and there isn't even a staircase leading up there. We have to climb a ladder that drops down from the ceiling, which she scurries up no problem; I take a bit more time.

The ladder leads us into the room through a hole in the ceiling, and Mina grabs my hand to help pull me up.

Her palm is warm against mine, like it was last night, and I almost reach to hold it again when she lets go and splays out on the floor.

I take in Mina's room, and I can feel her eyes on me as I look around. The ceilings are sloped, so I have to duck my head if I want to stand all the way up. There are string lights lining the angled walls, and wallpaper with animals pasted all over. Her bed has a million Squishmallows on it and the floor is covered in thick carpet that feels really nice against my feet.

"Your room is the best thing I've ever seen," I tell her as we sit on her carpet, cross-legged with our knees almost touching like we did in front of the fire.

"Thanks," she says, smiling as she looks around at her room. "It used to be the attic, but my mom agreed to let me sleep here and help me decorate it." She grabs a duck Squishmallow off her bed and hugs it to her chest. "We just renovated it this spring. It's pretty easy to get her to agree to stuff like that now, because of everything with the divorce."

"Oh."

I don't know what else to say. Beth and Alec were already divorced when I met Leo, so I've never seen what it's like when someone's parents are actively breaking up.

"Yeah." She shrugs. "It's whatever."

I get the sense that it's not *whatever,* but I don't push it. I don't want Mina to regret inviting me over.

Mina sits up on her knees then, and reaches above her

bed to a shelf. She pulls out a notebook, knocking over strips of medical tape in the process.

"Those are skin barriers for my stoma," she tells me. She must've seen me looking at the supplies. "It's to help make sure there aren't germs in the area of the hole or anything like that."

"Nice," I tell her. Because it is. I mean, that she's telling me all of this.

She drops the notebook next to me on the floor and then picks out some pens from her desk.

"What are you doing?"

"I always like to have a notebook nearby," she says. "What if we need to have a brainstorm session or something?"

"What would we need to brainstorm about?"

"I don't know, like, anything." She flips it to an empty page. "I love writing stuff down, especially animal facts and cool things that happen during the day or whatever. Aneliza says it's good because I have a lot to say."

We lie on our stomachs, while she shows me some of the animal facts that she wrote in the back of her notebook. Then we watch a five-minute video on her phone about tube worms. They're giant and weird, like white poles with something that looks like bright red lipstick sticking out of . . . some part of them.

"What if we measured people's heights by tube worms?" Mina asks, jumping up and laughing at her own idea. She pulls out a measuring tape. "Here, let's see how many tube worms tall we are."

I jump up too, ready to go along with whatever Mina says. She has me stand with my back against the wall, holding the tape measure steady with her foot as she stretches it up to my head. She bites her bottom lip in concentration, and I can feel her breath against my face as she checks the number.

I don't think I could move from this spot if I tried.

Mina lets the tape measure go, and it snakes back in on itself with a satisfying *thwack*; then she opens up the calculator on her phone. "You're a little more than three-quarters of a giant tube worm tall," she informs me.

I grin. "I feel like that's honestly super tall."

"Definitely more tube worms tall than me," she says, handing me the tape measure. "But let's check."

So, we do, and it's easier for me to measure her since she's way shorter than me. I let myself take a bit extra time to flatten my hand over her head and match it up with a number on the tape measure. The frizzy parts of her curls brush against my skin, and at that moment I feel a pang in my stomach that becomes overpowering.

"Actually, where's your bathroom?" I ask her quickly. "I really have to, like, go."

"It's right downstairs," she says as she grabs her notebook and writes something in it. "Take your time pooping."

I smile to myself as I climb down the ladder. It's as

simple as that: She knows I'm pooping, and she wants me to take my time.

She understands.

There's more medical equipment in the bathroom, like wipes, skin sprays, and silicone bags. The more Mina tells me about her ostomy bag, the more I want to know. Maybe it's because she has the same disease as me, or maybe it's because I want to learn everything about her and then make a note in my phone about her favorite songs and movies and ways to eat marshmallows.

Or something like that.

Once I'm back in her bedroom, Mina takes a turn down in the bathroom.

Then, when she's sitting next to me on the floor again, I clear my throat. "Can I ask you a question?"

"Is it about my colostomy bag?"

I nod. "How'd you know?"

"That's *always* what people wanna know, once they learn that I have it." She smiles. "It's fine, though, you can ask stuff. With other people I usually just send them videos that this YouTuber Hannah Witton makes. She's amazing." She turns to me. "But I'll tell you whatever you want to know. You get the inside scoop."

I have to look away as I ask, "So, you don't poop at all? Like, because of the bag?"

"I still poop," she says. "It just all goes into the bag. Plus all my farts go in there too, so no one can smell it when it happens because it's all trapped in there."

It's so easy for her to talk about this stuff. About poop and her body and maybe everything. If I had to have a colostomy bag, I definitely wouldn't want anyone to know about it. She's braver than me.

"But back before I had the bag, I was always running to the bathroom in the middle of class, and it was an emergency every time, but it never feels like that anymore. I just have to make sure I empty the bag so it doesn't get full."

"I'm always going to the bathroom during school too," I tell her, even though normally I'd be too embarrassed to talk about this. "And, like, the popular girls in my class laugh and stuff when I ask to go, and it sucks."

"Well, clearly they don't know how nice it can be to just sit in the bathroom and think for a while."

"Wait, yes!" I say. "It's literally the only time you can do whatever you want or look at whatever you want on your phone and no one can tell you not to."

She sits up and smiles at me. "That's actually so true. Before I had my bag, I used to carry a sign around with me that said 'Out of Order' that I could put on the bathroom door right before I ran in."

"You did?" I ask, laughing. "Did that actually work?"

"Oh, yeah," Mina tells me, looking proud. "Until someone called the custodian and she almost opened the stall door on me while I was pooping."

She starts laughing then too, and we're both cracking up. I try not to stare at her face while she laughs, at the way her eyes close and her mouth opens to show her front teeth. It's like she knows all the hacks for having Crohn's and for life too.

"You should talk about this kind of stuff at support group," she says. "These are the kinds of conversations I want us to have. Or, you know, you could talk about anything. I promise none of us will judge what you say."

"I know," I tell her. And I do. But so far, I've just wanted to listen to what everyone else is talking about. They all know so much more about being chronically ill and having IBD and I don't know what I'd have to add.

But then Mina says, "*I'd* like to hear what you have to say," and I'm suddenly planning what I'll talk about at the next meeting.

The moment is ruined, though, when I get a text from my mom telling me Beth is going to swing by to pick me up in a bit after she gets Leo from Peregrine's house. They've been hanging out more outside of rehearsal, which I'm trying not to think too much about.

"I have to go in a minute," I tell Mina, motioning to the text on my phone by way of explanation.

She frowns, rubbing her hand against the textured carpet. "Okay, but can we do this again soon, though? Like, hang out just the two of us?"

"That'd be really cool," I say.

"Yeah." She smiles at me. "It would."

I have a warm feeling in my stomach (good warm, not

poop-related) as we head down to the first floor. Once we're there, Mina has me say goodbye to Tarantula.

"She's telling me she's going to miss you," Mina says, putting her ear up to Tarantula's tank and pretending to translate.

"Tell Tarantula that she can always text me," I say, giggling.

Mina nods like Tarantula just whispered something to her. "She says 'will do.'"

And maybe it's just me looking for signs, but I could almost swear that after today, Mina has a crush on me too.

Chapter Sixteen

COOLEST KIDS IN THE HOSPITAL

"**It's not even** an important appointment," I tell my mom. We're driving to the hospital, and I have the next five minutes to convince her that she *absolutely* does not need to come into the examination room with me. "It's just a 'follow-up.'"

"I don't know, Al," she says. "I want to be able to ask Dr. Maltz questions."

"At my support group they said it's important for young adults such as myself to have privacy during our appointments." I hold my breath after I say it, waiting for a response. This isn't something Aneliza told us, it's just something Ethan mentioned on a FaceTime. He said it's his number one strategy for getting his mom off his back, even though Ms. Fienman is pretty great, as far as moms go.

My mom sighs as she pulls into the hospital parking lot. "Fine," she says. "I'll come into the room at the end of the appointment to ask my questions."

"Fine."

My mom finds a parking spot, and I run into the hospital lobby ahead of her.

"Al! How are you feeling?" Dr. Maltz asks as she walks into the examination room. It feels different to be in here without the fear of my mom butting in.

"Pretty good," I tell her, because honestly, I am. Crohn's-wise, at least.

"Have you noticed a difference in your stool?" Dr. Maltz asks while she washes her hands.

"There's definitely . . . less of it," I tell her, and she laughs in a way that makes me feel like I'm in on the joke. "And there's not as much blood."

I've heard how some of the other members of the Bathroom Club talk about their poop, so now I feel a tiny bit more comfortable telling Dr. Maltz about it.

"That's great," she tells me. "Both decreased frequency of bowel movements and the absence of blood can be a sign that the medicine is working."

Dr. Maltz does her usual routine—which unfortunately means sticking her finger up my butt yet again—and then sits in front of her little computer.

"I wanted to talk to you about something," she says, brushing a loose strand of hair back from her face. "Do you think we could bring your mom back in here?"

"Do we have to?"

"Until you're eighteen, unfortunately." She smiles. "I know it's unfair, but it's that pesky law."

I like that Dr. Maltz explains why she has to do something before she does it. A lot of grown-ups don't think to do that. It's usually "because I said so." But not with her.

"Before we bring your mom in, though, can I just ask you a couple of questions?"

I nod, but I know what's coming. My pediatrician started "asking me questions" last year. Like if I was doing drugs, or drinking alcohol, or other things that I can't imagine doing, ever.

But then Dr. Maltz says, "Has anything changed at home that might be causing you stress? I'm really happy with your improvements on the medication, but I'm still seeing a lot of blood."

"Um...hm..." *Liking a girl, her maybe liking me back, my best friend abandoning me for drama club.* "I don't think so," I tell her finally.

"Okay," she says with a gentle voice. "But just know that you can talk to me about absolutely anything. I know I'm your gastroenterologist, but your guts are connected to your brain, and I want to make sure that's okay too."

I wipe my eyes while she's typing something on the computer so that she can't see that her words made me tear up a little. My pooping *has* impacted more than just my butt, and I'm glad she cares about that too.

"Oh, by the way, did you end up going to the support group?"

"Yeah!" I tell her. This is something I actually *want* to talk about. "The people there are awesome."

"That's great," she says. "I thought you'd like them."

"I definitely do."

After that, Dr. Maltz calls my mom in, and I zone out thinking about how Dr. Maltz is also Mina's doctor (she treats everyone in the support group). I wonder what Mina thinks of her—mostly I wonder if she *also* thinks Dr. Maltz is kind of pretty.

"Did you hear what Dr. Maltz was saying?" my mom asks when we get home from the appointment. "There's a form she can sign that'll let you use the bathroom whenever you want. Can we take a look at it together?"

"What?" I ask, not really paying attention.

"It might be helpful so that you don't have to explain anything to your teachers. They'll be able to learn about your stomach problems from the form."

"I don't need that." It comes out really harsh, but I don't want my teachers getting some form that tells them exactly what's wrong with me. They'd know why I'm leaving class and what I'm doing in the bathroom. It's too embarrassing to even think about.

The next day is support group, which is great because it means I have somewhere to be after school, instead of waiting for Leo to get home from rehearsal like a sad puppy.

"I'm so happy to see you again, Al," Aneliza says as I

walk into the room. She's futzing with the refreshment table, and I wave to her happily. This time, I don't need her as a shield.

"Hey!" Carl waves me over.

I sit down next to him, and as I do, I can see that he's looking at Addison's latest post with her boyfriend, Hudson.

It's weird to think that Carl knows the same people that I do from school.

"Don't you think they're kind of annoying?" I ask, pointing to the little Addison on his screen.

He shrugs. "I don't really know them. But I used to be close friends with Hudson, back in like fourth grade."

My eyes go wide. "You were?" Hudson is top-tier cool, just like the Addisons.

"Yeah, but then we got to middle school, and I got sick, and we drifted apart, I guess. So, yeah."

"I'm sorry," I tell him.

"It's fine, I like the people here better anyway," Carl says, smiling at me.

I grin. "We're *way* better than Hudson and the Addisons."

"The what?" Carl asks.

My eyes go wide. I've never told anyone the name Leo and I have for Madison and Addison, mostly because I haven't had anyone to tell it to. "It's just a silly nickname my best friend and I have for Madison and Addison."

He snorts out a laugh as Mina hops into the room and meets my eye, then quickly looks away. I smile down at my shoes when she sits in the chair on my other side.

"Hey," she says.

"Hey," I say.

We both laugh for no reason. Her laugh sounds so, so nice, and it's amazing that she's laughing with me.

"All right," Aneliza says once everyone is settled. "Who wants to get us started?"

Mina nudges me, and just like that, my hand is in the air. Ever since she told me in her bedroom that she wanted to hear what I have to say, I've been excited to say *something* at support group. Even if it's not as good as what everyone else has to contribute.

"Al!" Aneliza says excitedly, probably because I didn't say anything at all last time. "Take it away."

"Um, I guess I just wanted to say that, like, I feel better with my medicine and stuff."

"That's great!" Aneliza tells me. "Sometimes finding the right medicine for you can be really frustrating, and I'm so happy to hear that it's working."

"Yeah, definitely." I shift a little in my seat. "But I guess it's also like, now I just ... *have* Crohn's, you know? Like it won't go away even though things are better?" I shrug. "And I feel like other people don't really get it since it's not something you can *see*? Like, if my stomach is better for a few days, then people might just think I'm *fine*, even if I'm not."

Aneliza nods. "That sounds really frustrating."

"It is," I say, picking at my nails. "Plus, my best friend's always at rehearsal for this show he's doing, so things are kind of different with him too."

I don't realize how much I've told the group until I stop talking. All of that just came out of me, like verbal diarrhea. Or . . . real diarrhea.

"Navigating friendships with a chronic illness can be really hard," Aneliza says, nodding sympathetically.

"Yeah," I say, staring at the stained floor.

"Can I add something?" Rikako asks.

Aneliza nods. "Of course."

"I just wanted to say that I'm also at the same rehearsals as Al's best friend, and he talks about you *all* the time." She looks at me as she says this. "He's always telling stories that start with 'One time, me and my best friend, Al . . .' It's kind of sweet."

"Really?" I ask.

Rikako nods. "Oh, yeah. And Leo's the best, by the way."

I smile at that, because obviously he is, and it's nice that other people think so too. And it's *also nice* that Leo's talking about me with his new friends, but now they all know about me. It's embarrassing to think about being the subject of conversation without knowing it, even if it's all good things.

No one else has much to say after that, so Aneliza takes control of the meeting. "I thought this week we could talk about boundaries." She glances around the room. "Do you ever have to set boundaries because of your IBD?"

"Sometimes I can't hang out with my friends because I know I'm just gonna be in the bathroom the whole time," Ethan says.

"That must be hard," Aneliza tells him. "Raise your hand if anyone else has had to set boundaries with friends recently because of your IBD."

At that, everyone raises their hand.

We discuss strategies for setting boundaries with friends when we're having a flare-up, and we all commiserate about pooping at a friend's house who doesn't have Crohn's or ulcerative colitis (not that I've done this with anyone except Leo, and even then I do my best to run back to my apartment).

When support group is over, we go out into the lobby to wait for pickup. We all sit in the spinny chairs that make me kind of nauseous, and I choose the one next to Mina.

I love the way it feels to hang out in the lobby, with doctors passing by and all the little kids who gape like we're the coolest people in the hospital. Which isn't saying much, but to me, it's everything.

Chapter Seventeen

MORE LIKE BUTTERFLIES THAN POOP

I'm FaceTiming the Bathroom Club later that night when Leo texts me.

LEO: my mom wants to talk w us

ME: why

LEO: idk can u just come over

ME: yea give me like 15 mins im facetiming my friends

Leo doesn't respond to that, so I keep playing Among Us. I never vote for Mina as the imposter, though. I watch our little guys running through the same ship together, doing tasks and getting ejected into space. I get that same feeling in my chest I always do when I'm playing games with the Bathroom Club, or with Mina—that I'm in the right place, even if that place is just my bedroom, staring at my phone.

And, okay, I obviously want Mina to like me back, but I don't think I could tell anyone about the two of us, even if something happened. I honestly can't decide if it would be worse for everyone to know about my poop or for everyone to know who I like, but either way I would combust like one of Mina's marshmallows.

After a few more rounds of Among Us, I tell the Bathroom Club I have to go (even though I *really* don't want to), and I head over to Leo and Beth's apartment.

"Hey, bubs," Beth says as I walk in. She's holding a couple of pieces of paper in her hand, but she has them face-down so I can't see what they say.

My arms are folded, and Leo's not looking at either of us.

"Lively bunch today, huh?" Beth asks sarcastically. But she perks up as she says, "Well, I've got a *huge* announcement that might help with those grouchy punims."

My stomach clenches up even though Beth's smiling. Grown-ups need to stop saying that they have a "huge announcement." Unless Beth found aliens in the back kitchen of the bakery, nothing's a "huge announcement" to me anymore.

Beth flips the pieces of paper over and hands one to each of us. "Voila!"

It takes me a minute to realize what it says, but once I do, I see that it's a ticket to see a musical on Broadway.

I turn to see Leo's reaction, but he's just standing there,

mouth open. "We're going to see *WICKED*??!!" he shouts after a minute.

Beth nods, grinning. "We sure are. All four of us." She points across the hall. "Your mom's coming too, Al!"

Leo and I share a quick glance; clearly neither of us expected this.

"Cool," I tell Beth, faking a smile as I think about what this means. We're all going to be in the city together for a full day. We'll have to take the train in early, then have a meal, see the show, and ride the train back. That's a lot of time for Leo to talk about how much he loves drama club, or for my mom to question everything I eat.

Beth grins. "This is going to be the best day ever!"

"Totally," Leo says, rocking back on his heels and smiling wide.

I don't say anything.

Later that night, I'm trying to work on a project for my science class about the bones of the human body when my phone lights up with a FaceTime request.

From Mina.

My first reaction is to throw my pencil across the room, then jump up and down. Because Mina is calling me. Just me.

"Hi?" I say when I pick up, hoping that Mina can't hear how loud my heart is beating right now.

"Al!" she says, like this is the most normal thing in the world. Like we FaceTime just the two of us every day.

She must be sitting on her bedroom floor, because she sets her phone down against something and then lies on the carpet, her chin in her hands.

"Um, so, what's up?" I ask when she doesn't say anything for a second.

She shrugs, but after a moment she blurts, "Do you think we'll hang out this summer?"

I try to look into her eyes, but she's tracing a pattern into the rug with her index finger. It's the first time I've seen her look anywhere *close* to nervous.

"We could roast marshmallows every day if we wanted," she continues, not looking up from the floor. "We could just hang out all the time this summer, really."

I slide down to the floor so that we're on the same level, even though we're not in the same place. It's like we're together here—she's joined me in the supercomputer realm. "I mean, yeah, we'll all hang out, right?" I ask. "Like, the whole Bathroom Club?"

"Well, maybe just you and me sometimes." She looks up at her phone now, and I look away, though I can't help the grin that spreads across my face.

My stomach clenches, and I try to hold in whatever I'm feeling, though it's more like butterflies than poop.

"We can keep measuring ourselves against giant animals," I say after a beat, trying my best not to let my phone shake along with my hands. "I bet I'm half a black bear tall, don't you think?"

"Oh, more than that," Mina says, laughing. "You're way too tall to only be half a bear." We're both quiet for a minute and then she says, "Al, can I tell you something?"

I might not have had to poop when Mina called, but I definitely do now. My stomach and my heart and my lungs and my entire body are going to explode.

"Um, okay?" I say, because what else *can* I say? When someone asks if they can tell you something, they're going to tell you no matter what.

"I like you, Al." She sits up and grabs her phone from where it was resting, so that her face is closer to the camera. "Like, *like* like you."

I'm so nauseous that if I opened my mouth, I would probably projectile vomit onto my phone.

"You don't have to say anything, obviously," she adds after an awkward few seconds. "I just wanted to let you know."

Holy.

Crap.

She came right out and said it. She told me she likes me.

I've liked girls for so long without anyone knowing, but now there's someone who needs to know.

I smile at that person, then take a deep breath and say it: "I like you too."

Chapter Eighteen

OUR TUBE WORM NAMED ALFRED

I've spent almost every waking hour today on the toilet.

Who knew that telling Mina I liked her back would make my bowels go into hyperdrive? Well, I guess I kind of knew. But, yeah.

It's different from poop emergencies before, though, because I almost like the way my stomach feels, all swoopy and fluttery. Plus, I get to text Mina while I'm pooping, and she doesn't even care that I'm texting from the toilet. She *likes* me. It's practically too much to believe.

Once I'm out of the bathroom, I fix my hair and lie down on my bed and make sure I'm holding my phone at the perfect angle.

Then I FaceTime Mina.

"Al!" she says, and I can see the string lights and wallpaper of her cozy attic bedroom in the background. I love how excited she sounds to say my name.

"Hi!" I immediately feel silly for getting into such a posed position on my bed, so I sit up and let a bit of my hair fall in front of my face.

Honestly, she's so cute that I'm a little overwhelmed. It's the first time I've spoken to her since we told each other about our feelings, and now I can't stop smiling.

She props her phone on a stack of books and grins back at me. "What's up?"

What's up?

Um, excuse me, Mina, I think PRETTY MUCH EVERYTHING is up. We LIKE EACH OTHER!!

"Not much, how about you?"

"I'm just hanging out," she says. "Wanna play a game?"

"Like what?"

"Well, we could try *this*," she says with a sly smile on her face as she pulls out a folded square of paper.

"What is it?"

"It's a fortune teller," she says, unfolding it and placing it over her fingers. "Have you used one?"

"Maybe?"

"Okay, so basically, you give me a color and a number, and I'll tell you your future."

"Any color? Any number?" I ask, and she nods.

"Okay, how about pink and five."

"Perfect." She spells out *P-I-N-K* as she folds the fortune teller four times, then folds it again as she counts to five. She shows me the folded triangle it landed on. "All right, should I open it?" I nod, and she unfolds the paper and reads: "You'll go to the moon and discover aliens."

She bursts out laughing, and I laugh too, then let out

a breath. I thought it would be something way more serious than that. "When I was little, I really wanted to be an astronaut," I tell her. "But I was too scared to actually go to space."

"Wait, really?" she asks. "Why? Space is awesome."

"No, it's terrifying! It literally never ends."

"That's what's so cool about it," she says. "It's like the bottom of the ocean, with the giant tube worms. No one knows anything about it!"

"Except *you* do," I tell her.

"Well, that's because I'm a genius," she jokes, sticking her tongue out. "I think I want to go to the bottom of the ocean more than space, though. That way we'd be the only people down there."

I grin. "Yeah, and we'd be best friends with the giant tube worm."

"Excuse me, his name is Alfred."

"Okay, sorry, we'd be best friends with Alfred."

I don't know how much I'd like to visit the bottom of the ocean, but maybe instead of that Mina and I can run away and move to another country and build a house with ten bathrooms and never speak to our parents again. I could go anywhere with her and I'd probably feel the same way I do now, all fluttery and safe.

I'm about to ask if she can do another round of the fortune teller when I hear my mom and Beth in the living room, and I freeze up.

I don't want them to overhear me talking to Mina now that there's something more going on between us. I want to keep her to myself.

So instead, I quickly say, "I gotta go, okay?"

"Sounds good," she tells me. "I'll keep myself busy planning our undersea expedition."

My heart hurts as she says this, because it's the best thing ever.

"I'll plan it too," I tell her, my voice lower now. "Can't wait to meet Alfred."

"Same." She grins at me. "Bye!"

I end the call while she's still waving goodbye.

Here's the thing: Maybe one day I *could* tell my mom about me and Mina, or at least about me liking girls. But right now the thought of her thinking of me as someone who has crushes and wants to kiss people and is more than just a floating brain connected to a supercomputer is mortifying.

I flop back on my pillow, open TikTok, and scroll through my FYP for a little while (on my backup account, obviously). I watch TikToks of people making these big earrings with farm animals on them and then one of a Chihuahua who has problems with his back legs so he runs in a silly way. I stop scrolling when a pretty girl with curly bangs and a pink bandana comes up on my For You page.

Talking to Mina is the only time I feel like all the parts of myself can exist at the same time. I don't have to hide being queer, and I don't have to hide having Crohn's, because Mina understands both. She's the only person I can talk to about absolutely *anything*, from our diarrhea to our dreams for the future. It's so nice to be in our little bubble, just the two of us playing games, tuning out the rest of the world.

So instead of worrying about anyone else, I send Mina a TikTok and wait for her response, phone clutched to my heart.

Chapter Nineteen

WE ARE NOT DEFYING GRAVITY

"That was the greatest thing my eyes have ever seen in my whole entire life," Leo says as we push through the crowd to find a table at the café. He's wearing the beanie his mom just bought for him at the merch stand that says DEFY GRAVITY, and he's *glowing*.

I grin at him, because honestly I'm still buzzing from the show too. I can't imagine wanting to be an actor like Leo, but seeing how much it takes for a musical to come together—the performers, the lights, the sets, the costumes—I think I'm starting to get why he loves it. He kept turning to me during the big numbers, and when he looked at me, it was like we were the Al and Leo Club again, even if it was just for the show.

"I'm glad you thought so, bubs," Beth says as one of the employees calls out her name to let us know our food is ready. "Ooh! I'll go grab our treats!"

"What'd *you* think, Allie?" my mom asks.

"It was really great," I admit.

My mom and I rarely come into the city, even though it's so close, and when we do, we never do touristy stuff like this. But today with Leo and Beth has been different, and I don't want the day to end. We saw a matinee, and now we're having dessert at this really cute café near the theater that Leo told us we *had* to go to.

"Peregrine said he eats there after every Broadway show he sees," Leo had told me on the train. "And he sees, like, so many. So, he's the expert."

I just nodded.

Beth returns to the table with four matcha cream puffs and two brown sugar tea lattes for me and Leo. We both wanted a fun drink, but our moms wouldn't let us have coffee, so this was the compromise.

"Did you know that *Wicked* has the shortest quick-change of any show on Broadway?" Leo asks as he scrolls through the *Wicked* Wikipedia page. "Elphaba only has fifteen seconds to change her dress."

I lean over to read along and let Leo's excited chatter wash over me. This is the most normal day I've had with him in a long time. Earlier, when we arrived at the theater, we snuck into the gender-neutral bathroom and took a million selfies, and our moms let us get M&M'S that we ate super quickly before the show so we "didn't disturb the cast," as Leo said. It was pretty great.

It's nice to hang out with him when he's not distracted by the show or Peregrine.

I take a sip of my drink, which is in a bowl-sized mug. The sugar makes my teeth hurt, so it's basically perfect.

"Remember to take it slow, Al. You don't want to overwhelm your stomach, do you?" my mom asks as we all start to dig into the cream puffs.

"Um, no?" I'm about to add something else, but when I look at her, she seems nervous. Maybe she's worried about not making our train home or something.

"Well, if the cream puff is too much for you to handle, we can always order something plainer."

"Mom, I'm fine," I say through gritted teeth.

I roll my eyes at Leo, but he's focused on the dessert.

"It's nice to be out of the bakery for a day," Beth says after a minute. "I'm *so* not used to people serving me."

My mom laughs much louder than usual, and I turn to Leo to try to see what he's thinking.

Then my mom clears her throat.

"So, there's actually a reason Beth and I wanted all of us to come to the city today."

The café is buzzing behind us, full of people laughing and discussing their favorite scenes from the shows they just saw.

"Like, other than the show?" Leo asks, smiling. "Is there another surprise?"

"Well," Beth says, laughing a little. "Not the kind you're expecting, I don't think."

My stomach begins its revolt, gurgling and spluttering in the way I just promised my mom it wouldn't.

"So, what is it?" I want to get this over with.

Beth smiles at my mom, and then does something that makes my already gurgling stomach even worse: She wraps an arm around her waist.

"We've been wanting to tell you two bubs for a while now," Beth says, gazing at my mom and smiling. My mom doesn't smile back, though; her face is stony and pale.

She seems scared.

Beth takes a breath. "What we wanted to say is this: We're dating." She looks across the table at me and Leo. "Joanna and I are together."

"Wait, like, you're a couple?" he asks.

"Yeah, bubs," Beth says.

I can tell that Leo's looking over at me, but right now my lap is the most interesting thing in the world. I can't meet anyone's eyes.

My mom likes girls. She's queer.

She's . . . like me.

I was just FaceTiming Mina *yesterday,* worried that my mom would overhear, that she would know I like someone. And all along my mom *also* likes someone, a *woman* someone, in the same way that I like Mina.

It's too much. I want to run to the bathroom, but I'm frozen. My eyes dart around the café—I still try to locate the restrooms, just in case.

"I think it's cool," Leo says, and I can hear the smile in his voice. It feels like a betrayal.

No, no no.

He only thinks it's "cool" because he's never felt what I feel. He's never had to create a backup TikTok to watch videos of girls kissing in secret. *Cool* is the last word I would ever use.

"Thanks, Leo," my mom says. I bet she's looking at me, waiting for me to say something.

But I won't. I can't. Because there's one thought, louder than all the rest in my brain, louder than the gurgling in my stomach: *I can never tell.*

I can never tell anyone that I like girls. They'll think I'm copying my mom. They'll think I'm lying. They'll think I'm a freak. They'll think it's contagious.

I push my cream puff away and sink down in my seat.

"We can talk about this more later, but we just thought it was important for you two to know," my mom says after a minute. "We're still going to live in our own apartments. I promise, this won't change anything."

I almost laugh at that.

Because, of course, it changes everything.

Chapter Twenty

CLOWN TORTURE AND KID WEDDINGS

"Alison, Leonard, get your head in the game!" Mr. DiMeglio shouts at us as we half-heartedly throw balls in the air and try to catch them.

We're doing a juggling unit in gym now, which I don't think is a real thing, but Mr. DiMeglio's obsessed with the circus. He keeps trying to demonstrate by showing how many balls he can throw in the air at once. His max is three and then he starts dropping them.

I pick up one of the multicolored juggling balls and throw it in the air, but it lands on the floor halfway across the gym.

I'm feeling . . . off today, like I'm just going through the motions. I woke up, I got myself to school, made it to gym class—but nothing feels real.

I think I'm in shock.

"So, like, did you know anything was going on?" Leo asks after a minute.

Whenever we've talked about it today, Leo and I have

avoided specifics. It's an unspoken pact, that we're keeping this a secret.

At least, that's what *I* think we're doing.

"Nope," I tell him as I toss the bean-filled juggling ball from hand to hand.

"So, I guess *that's* why they've been trying to get us to hang out more," Leo says. "Because they wanted to test things out."

I shrug. "I guess."

Things feel weird between me and Leo today too; we can't seem to meet each other's gaze.

"Eyes on the prize," DiMeglio shouts at us as he walks by. "Eyes on the prize."

Our moms told us we could take a "mental health day" from school if we wanted, but neither of us did. The idea of staying home with them and discussing our feelings (ew) was the worst thing imaginable.

"What were you and your mom talking about last night?" I ask Leo. "Like, after we got home?"

The only thing my mom asked when we got home was if my stomach felt okay from the cream puffs. Not "How do you feel about me dating Leo's mom." Not "Surprise! I like women." Just a stomach check-in, then she went to her room. The worst part was that I could *hear* Beth and Leo laughing across the hall.

He gazes down at the ball in his hand. "You know, stuff."

"Well, yeah," I say. "But what *kind* of stuff?"

"Just stuff, okay?" he snaps.

I nod, turning away from him.

After a minute, Leo sighs and adds, "Something she told me was that she wants us all to feel like a family eventually."

I almost roll my eyes at that, because I have no idea how it'll ever happen, or how we'd ever feel comfortable together like that now that we know our moms are dating. It's different from when they were friends, because our lives still felt separate. Now everything is blending together.

The Addisons run around the gym pretending to juggle, but really they're just flirting with the popular boys in our class. When they pass in front of us they slow their jog down a bit, staring at us curiously but not saying anything.

I hate that they think they can be in everyone's business just because they're cool and tiny and the eighth-grade boys like to pick them up and spin them around on the back fields.

They're part of the reason why I'm super worried about people finding out that my mom is dating Beth.

Back in kindergarten, I was actually friends with Madison (aka half of the two-headed Addisons monster). We always played this game where we would pretend to get married to each other and dress up and play music and sing songs and promise to love each other forever and ever.

But one day at school Addison caught Madison and me

playing wedding at recess, and she couldn't stop laughing at the fact that we had pretended to marry each other.

Madison and I never played wedding or family after that. And we stopped being friends when we were in different classes in first grade, but I still think about it sometimes. About her, walking down the fake aisle in her fake wedding dress. About how it might be nice if it was real. If one day I got to marry a girl and watch her walk down the aisle.

What if my mom and Leo's mom will do more than just date? What if they get *married*?

Maybe Addison will laugh at that too.

Her laughter rings out now, through the gym. We're halfway through class; I can't seem to catch a single ball. Juggling is a torture method invented by clowns to make children feel inadequate.

Leo's just as distracted. I throw the ball up in the air again, and it hits him on the head.

"Sorry!" I tell him, but he barely notices. All he does is pick it up and hand it back to me. "Thanks."

"Mhm."

DiMeglio blows his whistle, and we switch from the station we're at to a station where we have to try to juggle with these big red rings.

"Wanna know something?" Leo asks me quietly after a minute.

"What?"

"This girl who's in the ensemble of the show has two dads." He looks up at me. "Isn't that cool?"

"Yeah, I guess."

"I thought maybe we could, like, talk to her or something."

"Why?"

"Because she *has two dads.*" Leo whispers the last part. "*Who are gay.*"

"*I don't even have* one *dad,*" I whisper back, rolling my eyes.

I know it's mean, but I don't know what else to say. There's no way I'm talking to some random girl I don't even know about her gay dads. Plus, her situation is completely different from ours. Her dads have probably been there since she was a baby or a young kid at least.

I don't understand how Leo can't see that our situation is different. It's too new to talk about with his drama club friends, who are complete strangers to me.

"You didn't tell her, though, did you?" I ask him.

Leo shakes his head and crosses his arms, which makes it impossible to throw the rings into the air at all.

"Less talky, more juggle-y!" DiMeglio yells at us from across the gym.

I throw the ring up so high and hard that I practically send it into orbit.

Chapter Twenty-one

IT'S NOT THE CREAM PUFFS

We're back in Ethan's basement, and Mina's sitting right next to me on the couch.

I'm trying not to be nervous, but I can't stop myself from thinking about how I felt when she told me she liked me. How it made my stomach churn and my cheeks flush.

But thinking about *that* just makes me think about my mom, and how her relationship with Beth probably started as a crush. She's felt these same feelings before; she's thought about Beth like I've thought about Mina. Maybe her heart almost stopped when Beth first said she liked her.

Everything about being a human feels overwhelmingly embarrassing.

So far tonight, we've been watching another old movie that Carl recommended. This one's about a popular girl who tries to make this other girl cool, and also she's in love with her stepbrother. That last part is weird, but the movie's pretty good.

I start to lose track of the plot, though, because every five minutes I have to get up from the couch and go to the bathroom.

Ever since my mom and Beth revealed their big news over matcha cream puffs, my stomach's been out of control, just like everything else in my life. It's like my body has its own thoughts about all of *this*. It wants me to sit on the toilet by myself and poop and poop and poop. And there's a ton of blood in my stool (as Dr. Maltz would say).

"Are you all right?" Rikako asks after what must be my tenth time getting up to poop.

Carl pauses the movie, clearly a little annoyed that we're talking.

"Um, yeah," I say, sitting back next to Mina, who slides her leg closer to mine.

Did anyone notice?

"If you're pooping a ton, you might be having a flare-up," Ethan says while eating a giant pretzel stick. I haven't felt hungry enough to even touch the snacks his mom bought for us, which is super unfair since my stomach must be completely empty by now with all the times I've pooped.

Rikako and Carl nod, and Mina doesn't look at me as she adds, "You should honestly make an appointment with Dr. Maltz. She can adjust your medicine."

I try to catch her eye, but she's staring at the paused TV.

"Maybe," I say to them, even though the last thing I want to do is tell my mom that my stomach is getting worse.

Mina brushes her thigh up against mine, and it starts to feel like I have a separate stomach in my leg, one that's gurgling and churning with a vengeance.

And then my actual stomach gurgles, and I have to run up to the bathroom. Which isn't awkward in and of itself, because everyone in the Bathroom Club has run out of the room for a poop-mergency, but Mina will think it's because of her leg touching mine. And I guess it kind of is.

Ms. Fienman has stocked the bathroom with crosswords and magazines, but I forgo those in favor of my own anxious thoughts.

Maybe Mina thinks that dating each other is a terrible idea, and my stomach knows before my brain, like a poop-based premonition.

As I sit here spiraling, the toilet fills up with more and more of my, uh, *anxieties,* until I'm doubled over in pain and even emptier than before.

Ethan has one of those toilets that lets you choose the flush-level when you poop or pee, but it needs a setting that's something like "tsunami," because even the poop setting isn't cutting it.

The more I try to flush, the worse it gets, and there's no plunger to be found, which, if I'm honest, seems like an oversight on Ms. Fienman's part when she knows her son has IBD and is hanging out with a group of kids who also have it.

I do what I can to clean up, but when I tell Ms. Fienman

what happened, she insists it's "not a problem" and that it "happens all the time."

When I go back downstairs, no one comments on my absence. But half of my brain is upstairs with the toilet, and the other half is down here with Mina, who's once again inches from me.

The last thing I want is to see my mom right now, but when our agreed upon pickup time comes, Ms. Fienman comes outside with me to explain the situation to her.

"Why didn't you tell me you weren't feeling well?" she asks as we're driving back to our apartment. "I would've made an appointment with Dr. Maltz." She sighs. "And I definitely wouldn't have let you eat those cream puffs after the show."

It wasn't the cream puffs, I want to tell her. *Stop with the cream puffs! It was* you!

Instead of saying that, though, I just roll my eyes. Of course my mom is back to babying me. But at least we're talking—things have been super awkward between us since the news.

"I didn't think my stomach was that bad," I say finally, in response to her question.

"Clearly it's bad if you clogged Ms. Fienman's toilet, Al."

I cross my arms. "It's fine. It's whatever."

She sighs and looks over at me. "You're not allowed to be a teenager yet. You're not even thirteen."

I don't even have the words to explain how mad that

makes me. I'm dealing with a lot. Probably more than most thirteen-year-olds. She can't say I'm not allowed to be a teenager when in the past few weeks I've had a colonoscopy, found out I have a disease that will never go away, and told a girl I like her.

"Whatever," I say, crossing my arms.

"See?" my mom says, not quite joking, and I want to scream.

But first, I have to poop.

When I'm on the toilet, I pull out my phone, and there's a whole string of texts from Mina.

MINA: i hope ur feeling ok!!
do u want me to send u worm pics to make u feel better??

I bite my lip and stare up at the bathroom ceiling. Even though things were weird, she's still checking in on me. She cares if I'm okay.

ME: yes but only if they're not super gross

MINA: AL WHAT
how dare u!!!
all worms are pretty

ME: if u say so. . . .
i trust ur worm judgment

MINA: but they're not as pretty as u 😊

My stomach reacts to the text instantaneously and sends another bout of poop into the toilet.

I don't know how she can be so brave, especially when we barely talked at Ethan's. I want her to know I saw the text, and that I think she's pretty too—maybe the prettiest person ever—and that I want to hang out with her more and measure ourselves against animals and hear her talk about her bag for hours.

But instead of telling her any of that, all I can get myself to send back is: 💗

I hope she'll understand.

Chapter Twenty-two

SPECIAL MOMENTS IN THE INFUSION SUITE

Thanks to Ms. Fienman's clogged toilet, I had an appointment with Dr. Maltz today, only three days after the latest poop incident.

My mom is filling out the post-appointment paperwork, and I'm trying not to focus too much on what Dr. Maltz told me. She said that Crohn's and anxiety can go hand in hand (which, duh) and that to manage my symptoms I need to manage my anxiety.

Not so simple.

My mom puts on her reading glasses to better see the forms, when I get a text.

MINA: are u still at the hospital?

I told her last night that I had my appointment today. And she wished me luck and sent me a heart emoji, which nearly made my own heart burst.

ME: lol yeah i'm here!!
just got out of the exam room

MINA: im here too!!!!! they moved my appointment up
im getting my medicine
can u come to the infusion suite or do u have to leave
right away?
it's just on the other side of the floor from gastro

When I look up from my phone, my mom and Dr. Maltz are shaking hands. I thank her for her advice about reducing my anxiety (even if it's literally impossible given, well, everything) and then tell my mom I'm going to the bathroom.

"It might take a while," I say when we're out of earshot of Dr. Maltz.

And then I run.

I rush across the hall to the infusion suite, and by the time I get there I'm out of breath and I really do feel like I'm about to poop my pants.

The door to the room is closed and the glass is frosted, so I can't see if Mina's in there.

ME: im right outside lol

I try to sound cool and chill, even though I'm definitely not cool or chill and I certainly won't be if my mom finds out I'm not in the bathroom *and* that I'm trying to visit the girl I have a crush on in the infusion suite.

But before I can worry too much, Mina's there standing in front of me, looking so unfairly cute in her choker with hearts on it and a baby-doll T-shirt, even with the needle poking out of her arm. Now I'm not thinking about my mom at all.

"Hi!" she says.

"Hi," I say.

We smile at each other for so long my cheeks hurt.

She wheels her infusion bag so it's not blocking the door. "Do you wanna come in?"

"Is that okay?"

She gestures for me to look inside the room. Other than a nurse who's busy on a computer, no one's there.

The walls are lined with big comfy recliners, and Mina sits in one. She puts her feet up, and I perch on the edge of the chair next to hers.

The room is loud, with machines buzzing and beeping in the background, but Mina doesn't say anything.

"How come you need to get an infusion?" I ask after a minute.

"It's because I take Remicade," she says, sitting up a little. "They give it to me to make sure my symptoms don't come back."

"Even though you have the bag?"

"Yeah, it's just, like, a precaution, I guess."

I nod, but what I really want to do is ask, *So, are we dating??* Because we've both told each other that we *like* like the other, and maybe that's what comes next. I don't even know if she still likes me even though we both literally said the words "I like you" to each other. But maybe she doesn't feel that way anymore.

"How long do you have to stay here?" I ask instead.

She slams her head back against the chair and looks over at me. "Two *hours.*"

"That sucks."

"Well, at least you're here," she says, leaning closer to me.

Just then, the nurse comes by to check on Mina and offer her a juice box.

"No thanks," she tells her. Once the nurse is gone, Mina pulls the armrest up on her chair, and then does the same for mine. Now it's like our recliners are a couch. She scoots closer to me, then adjusts her IV. I hold my breath.

"So," she says quietly. "Remember when I told you about how I like . . . *like* you?"

I nod. Maybe my thoughts were so loud that she could hear them. Now I'm wishing I *had* stopped in the bathroom before I came here. Mina is much braver than me to bring this up at all; I'd probably just think about it for the rest of my life and never do anything.

"Of course," I tell her. "Remember when I told you I *like* like you too?"

We both laugh at that, like we're in on the best secret in the universe. Then I take a deep breath and try to stop my stomach from yelling at me as I ask, "But, like, what does this mean?" I look down. "That we both *like* like each other?"

Mina puts her hand on top of mine, and I meet her eye.

"You keep asking stuff like that," she says, and I must look confused, because she adds, "We should both just *do* stuff sometimes, you know?"

Mina's so bold in a way I don't know how to be, even when it's just the two of us.

I really *do* know what she's saying, though. But I also know that when I *do* things, like poop a million times at Ethan's house, or play pretend wedding with Madison, there are consequences.

So, it's better to just *not*.

But on the other hand, she's so pretty. She's probably the prettiest girl I've ever seen in my entire life, and she's taught me about worms and measured me against them. She smells like roses and she lets me see her ostomy bag. I've watched way too many TikToks and YouTube videos where girls kiss. I know what it's supposed to look like.

It's just that I have no idea how to do it myself.

But I want to show Mina that I'm brave.

"Um, Mina?" I ask.

She tilts her head at me. "Yeah?"

"Would it be okay if I, like . . ." I look down. "Do you think I could maybe kiss you?" I ask quietly.

I live a whole eternity before she nods.

She moves the IV, and I lean in. I close my eyes and the moment her lips press against mine, my body feels like it will explode.

Maybe this is why I'm not a supercomputer attached to a brain; so that I can feel this.

The kiss is nothing like the TikToks I've seen. It's better because it's mine. We only kiss for a couple of seconds, but her mouth is warm, and if we weren't at the hospital or if my body weren't shaking like a magnitude ten earthquake, I would want to stay here for a long, long time.

After we break apart, we smile at each other.

"Was that okay?" she asks, and I almost laugh because I could ask her the same exact thing.

"That was more than okay," I tell her. "It was amazing."

She leans back in and pecks my cheek, pushing her IV line out of the way yet again. I place my hand on the spot where her lips touched my skin, grinning.

For once, I told someone what I was really feeling. I let it out.

And for once, it was perfect.

"Definitely," she says.

I take a deep breath. It's like my body is filled with air and I could float up to the ceiling of the infusion suite.

"So," I say, trying not to smile too hard.

"So what?" Mina asks, reaching her knee out to touch my leg.

I know what I want to ask, but it's too scary, so I just shrug.

"You can say it," Mina whispers.

I lean in close to her. "Are we kind of like . . . girlfriends?"

When I pull back, she grins at me, then nods. "Yeah," she says. "I think so."

"Cool," I say, so relieved I almost pass out. Which would work out fine because we're in a hospital. It's actually the safest place to ask your crush to be your girlfriend, if you think about it. Because if you *do* pass out from relief, a nurse can come by and wave some smelling salts in your face or whatever it is they do to wake people up.

"How much longer do you have in here?" I ask Mina, pointing to her IV. I don't want to leave her here while she's getting her medicine. Not after our kiss.

She shrugs. "Probably like another hour, but I don't know if my mom or my dad is picking me up, so I might have to wait."

"Do they live in different places?" I ask, remembering what she said about them getting counseling and all of that.

She nods. "Yeah, my dad got an apartment across town a few months ago." She looks over at me. "But on the bright side, he bought me, like, ten Squishmallows when he moved, so that's cool."

I'm not sure if I should laugh at that, but she does, so I smile a little.

Then she turns her gaze to the infusion suite floor. "I just wanted to say that it's been really cool to have the

Bathroom Club while this is happening," Mina says. "And especially you. When you were over at my house, it was like none of that mattered."

My stomach twists at that, but not in the way it does when I'm anxious. I'm still learning about all the messages my stomach sends me, but I think this one is part of having a crush on Mina.

Right as I'm about to reply, my mom sends me a text. Because of course she'd ruin the best moment of my life.

MOM: Are you still in the bathroom?

ME: almost done

It's only been like fifteen minutes, but everything with Mina is different. I mean, we just *kissed,* and she told me about her parents.

I'm leaving this room a changed Al. A better one. One with a *girlfriend.*

"I have to go," I tell Mina. "But can we FaceTime later? And I'll text you a ton while you're finishing your treatment."

She smiles. "Yeah! Definitely."

"Okay, cool."

I run out of the infusion suite, sneak into a nearby bathroom, and try not to squeal too loudly when I shut myself in the stall. I shake out my hands and legs and do a little dance.

MINA AND I KISSED! I KISSED MINA! AND IT WAS INCREDIBLE!

I take as many deep breaths as I can to calm down, and when I walk out a minute later, my mom's heading down the hall toward me.

"You doing okay, Al?" she asks, smoothing out my hair.

I don't know how to tell her that every day, things get more complicated. That maybe I was doing okay a year ago, or a month ago, or even a week ago. But now things are amazing and scary and complicated and beyond my ability to communicate to her.

So I just say "Yup!"

Chapter Twenty-three

FLOATING BRAIN VIBES ONLY

I have the perfect after-school routine now: Run to my room, slam the door, and text Mina.

> ME: wait this quiz is so rude
> what did u get

Mina sent me a link to a "Which Terrifying Deep Sea Creature Are You?" quiz and I got the giant isopod, which is super gross-looking.

> MINA: anglerfish 🐟

> ME: ugh of course
> that one's the most iconic

I love flirting with Mina from the privacy of my own room. I still can't believe that we're dating, because she's the coolest person ever. She sends me selfies and pictures of her tarantula and TikToks and I don't know what I did to deserve all that. I try to send her some selfies too but I'm always worried that my face looks weird or that the lighting's off.

MINA: brb going to the bathroom

ME: aren't u gonna take ur phone?????

I'm only asking because it's sort of par for the course for people to say that they're on the toilet in the Bathroom Club group chat. It's one of my favorite things about our messages, that they're different from the way I talk to everyone else. We can talk about our poops, or our stomachs hurting, or gas pain, and it's not a joke. It's just, like, telling our friends about our lives.

There's the rest of the world, and then there's the Bathroom Club.

MINA: i have to empty my pouch lol 💀

ME: right yes cool!!!
text me when ur done:0

MINA: of coursssssseeeee

I sometimes forget that Mina doesn't poop the same

way I do, especially when we're not face-to-face. It's almost like I forget we're actual people at all, and not just the words we send back and forth to each other. It's as close as I can get to just being a floating brain, which is nice.

Now that I know Mina won't text back for a minute, I scroll through my backup TikTok, liking videos of other queer kids with abandon. I recognize myself in them even more; the smiles when they talk about their crushes, their descriptions of their first kiss.

This feels like yet another separate part of my life, and I love it. I send a TikTok to Mina of two girls in middle school playing truth or dare and saying they like each other. That's literally us, I tell her.

And it is, but only when I'm talking to her from the comfort of my room, or in the infusion suite. When other people—namely, my mom—factor into the equation, I don't know what to think.

I'm about to send another TikTok to Mina when my mom (of course) knocks on my door.

"Can I come in?" she asks, already most of the way into my room.

I scramble to shove my phone under my pillow and sit on my bed, cross-legged.

"How's it going in here?" she asks, leaning against the wall next to the door frame.

I just shrug. She almost never comes into my room like this. I thought we had an unspoken agreement that my room is the place where she can't bother me, where she can't tell me what to eat and how to live.

She wrings her hands together, staring at my carpeted floor. "I just wanted to check that you didn't want to—I mean, I know you must have questions, and"—she takes a shaky breath—"you don't want to talk about what Beth and I told you and Leo the other day, do you?"

My heart stops, but my stomach's in overdrive. She obviously doesn't want to talk about it, and I *definitely* don't, so I shake my head. "I'm okay."

She seems relieved. "Okay, great," she says, turning to leave. "Beth said I should check."

I want to roll my eyes at that. Of course Beth had to tell my mom to have a conversation with me that's not about my stomach.

"Well, don't forget to take your medicine, okay?"

Aaand there it is.

"Remember what Dr. Maltz said?" my mom asks. "One missed day really does make a difference. You could have another flare-up."

"I won't," I say through gritted teeth.

Then my mom lets the door close behind her, but it doesn't shut all the way, so I stomp over to make sure it's good and shut.

I flop back on my bed and grab my phone. Even though I never *ever* want to talk to my mom about her and Beth, I do wish sometimes that we had the kind of relationship that Beth and Leo have, where they can talk to each other about anything and everything. Where love isn't filtered through worry.

MINA: im back
what'd i miss

ME: just my mom being annoying

MINA: loll oh no

ME: my mom's just really on me about taking my meds
like obviously im gonna take them
you know?

MINA: yeah
but it's cool that she like pays attention to that kind of stuff

ME: do ur parents not?

MINA: nah
like they know when my infusions are
but mostly they're too distracted by like
counseling and stuff

ME: im sorry mina

that sounds terrible
but im here to talk if u want

I really do mean it; I want to be someone she can trust. I want her to tell me about animals that live where they shouldn't survive and her parents' counseling sessions and I want it all to feel normal, like it would if we were dating.

Which we are.

I'm dating Mina. I grin to myself for longer than I mean to.

MINA: we should talk about this at support group

ME: our parents???

MINA: yea!
i mean i will if u will

ME: hmmm
really? u want to?

Support group is a safe space with just me and the Bathroom Club and Aneliza. It's our group chat, but in person. We talk about poop, and our feelings, but not usually big family stuff. Or, at least, I haven't. If I brought up my mom, it would make support group feel different. I don't want to think about her while I'm there.

But then I see Mina's next text.

MINA: please ☹️

ME: lol fine
but u have to start the convo

MINA: yay!
im emailing aneliza now
she'll be so excited that i suggested a topic

I shake my head; I can't say no to Mina. If she wanted me to dive down to the bottom of the sea with her without an oxygen tank, I'd still say yes.

After that, we talk a little bit more, just texting silly things back and forth.

MINA: i gotta go to sleep
but i'll see you at support group!

When I check the time, it's somehow 11:00 p.m. I've been talking to Mina for hours, and I haven't even needed to get up to go to the bathroom or get water or do anything to keep my body functioning.

ME: goodnight!!!!!

MINA: night al

I feel all warm and tingly seeing Mina write my name out like that, and I fall asleep a few minutes later, hoping that I dream of nothing else but her.

Chapter Twenty-four

MOMS AND DADS AND PARENTS, OH MY

"Dude no, absolutely not," Ethan says at this week's support group. "If you tell me you like mint chocolate chip ice cream, I don't know what I'll do. Like, we can't be friends anymore."

Carl looks offended. "I don't like it," he tells Ethan. "I *love* it."

Ethan groans, and everyone around the circle laughs.

"Why don't we get back to the topic at hand?" Aneliza asks. "*Parents.*"

The knot in my stomach tightens, even though I knew this was coming. I was still kind of hoping that instead we might talk about something easier to digest like "anxiety" or "medicine" or "venomous snakes."

Anything would be better than this.

"I'll go," Ethan says. "My mom is literally the best—like you all know she's great—" Mina whoops at this as if she's cheering for Ms. Fienman at a baseball game. "But I guess I sometimes feel like she worries about me more than she needs to."

I nod along to that.

"Did you want to respond to Ethan, Al?" Aneliza asks, and I shake my head. Mina stares at me, but I shrug. I can't talk about my mom right now. I don't even know if I can speak.

"Thank you for sharing, Ethan." Aneliza leans forward. "Seems like that's something some of our other support group members can relate to. Having a kid with a chronic illness can be scary for parents too, but that's not on you to worry about."

I don't nod this time, because I don't want Aneliza to see I agree and ask me to speak, but I really, really understand what she's saying. Even if Crohn's is scary for my mom, her response shouldn't be showing me how worried *she* is. It shouldn't be telling me what to eat and monitoring my stomach. I'm not a baby, and I'm the one who actually *has* a chronic illness.

But, looking around the group, I don't think I can tell them. I *want* to; I want to say something. Except my heart is beating too fast and my stomach is clenched, and right before I'm about to run out of the room, Mina raises her hand, meeting my eye as she does. I'm grateful for the distraction.

"I guess it's just kind of weird that my parents are getting divorced, because my stomach was really bad when they started fighting, and now it's better, but, like, their relationship isn't." She takes a breath. "I feel kind of guilty about how much better I feel, because my mom is crying all the time and my dad barely wants to see me and my brother doesn't understand how bad everything is."

Aneliza nods sympathetically. "Thank you for sharing, Mina." She leans forward. "Do you think that *they* might be better too, though? Has their relationship seemed better now that they live in separate places?"

I look away as Mina wipes away tears and nods. "I *know* they're better." She sniffles, then says, "I just wish they could work things out. Then my stomach would be better and my parents would be better—" She turns to me and smiles a little. "I'd pretty much have the perfect life."

I can't believe how brave Mina's being. Or, well, I guess I can, because that's who she is. But hearing her talk like that about her parents makes me want to show her that I can do the same. That I can be vulnerable and talk to our friends about what's going on.

I want to know about every single aspect of her life, and it seems like Carl and Ethan and Rikako want to as well. Or at least none of them are put off by what Mina was saying.

These four people are some of my best friends, and I want to be honest with them. But no one except for Leo knows that my mom is dating a woman. Mina doesn't even know that my mom's dating *anyone*. But I promised her I'd contribute.

I just have to work my way up to it.

Carl goes next, and he talks about how things have been

tense between his parents since they're preparing for his bar mitzvah. He sits back in his chair and lets out a long sigh when he's done.

I tried to smile and nod as he was talking, but inside I'm wondering why it seems so much easier for everyone else to share than me. Maybe it's because they have more practice; or maybe I'm just worrying too much.

"Thanks for sharing, Carl," Aneliza says. "Would anyone else like to go? It doesn't have to be about Crohn's or ulcerative colitis. We're here for *whatever* you're going through. Right, team?"

Everyone nods, so I do too. I *am* here for everyone. But I don't know if everyone would be here for me if they knew I was hiding this huge thing from them. I want to be open, but I've spent so long keeping my thoughts inside that it feels like it's too late.

So I'm not going to tell them the whole truth—the part about my mom dating Beth—but I'm going to do what I promised Mina.

I take a breath and look over at her. She gives me an encouraging smile, and I try to smile back, but I think it probably makes me look constipated, which is the opposite of how I feel. I feel like I might have explosive diarrhea at any second.

But Mina's encouraging me. I want to do this for her, for this loud girl who loves worms and who *likes* me. For my girlfriend.

I raise my hand and Aneliza gestures for me to talk. "So, like, my stomach's kind of been worse." I shrug, hoping that Aneliza will comment on that and then move on, but she just nods—her signature move. "And, like, I think it's partially because of something with my mom." I look over at Mina. I didn't even tell her this part, but I can't chicken out now. "She's actually . . . dating someone."

My stomach gurgles as I say it, and I want to run out of the room.

But Aneliza leans forward. "That sounds like a really big change, Al," she says, then goes on to tell everyone that big life changes can cause our disease to flare up, even if we don't want it to.

Mina's staring at me, and I try to figure out what she's communicating through her glance, but I don't understand her expressions yet the way I do Leo's—or did.

The group is quieter than normal as we walk out into the lobby of the hospital, maybe because today's support group felt heavier than ones we've had in the past. When we reach the sliding glass doors to the parking lot, Mina pulls me aside, away from the group.

"Your mom is *dating* someone?" she asks, playing with the edge of her phone case.

I nod. "Yeah."

"I didn't even know your parents were divorced," Mina says, sounding kind of excited. "When did it happen? How come you didn't tell me?"

"No, no," I tell her, even though weirdly right now I wish they *were* divorced because I want to be able to have the same experience as Mina, or to talk her through it. "My parents aren't divorced. I mean, they were never married, and I don't really know my dad."

Mina's eyes go wide. "I'm sorry, I just assumed." Then she furrows her brows. "I thought maybe you would've told me that, like, when I talked about my parents last night when we were texting? It's fine that you didn't, obviously, I just . . ."

"I wanted to tell you," I say quickly. I really *do* want her to know everything about me, it's just that *everything* is too much and mortifying and no one, not even Leo, knows the full story.

I feel almost desperate now. I don't want to keep this from Mina, that my mom is dating Beth. She knows everything else about me, and, at least so far, I don't think she thinks I'm too much.

I mean, she's queer and has Crohn's too, so she gets that part, at least.

So, I make a decision. "If I tell you something, will you promise not to tell *anyone*? Not even Rikako or Carl or Ethan?"

Mina nods, then holds out her pinkie. "Pinkie triple dog giant tube worm promise."

I smile a little, and hook my pinkie in hers.

"My mom's actually dating Leo's mom."

I hold my breath and clench my stomach, and, for a moment, Mina doesn't say anything. I want to flush myself down a toilet. This is it; the end of our relationship.

Then she breaks out into a grin and hugs me.

"THAT'S AMAZING!" she shouts.

I look around at the hospital lobby, making sure that no one here heard her, though the only people around right now are doctors.

I smile a tiny bit. "It is?"

"Yes! We can have Leo's mom's biscochos whenever we want now!" Mina says, speaking quickly. "And we can all hang out!"

Even as Mina's talking about these things, I can't picture them. Because one thing I absolutely positively will not be doing is telling my mom that I have a girlfriend. She doesn't know I'm queer—she barely knows anything about me other than the fact that my stomach hurts.

Mina doesn't stop smiling even as my mom picks me up outside the hospital, and I try to smile too, but it must look more like a grimace.

Because all I want to do is throw up.

Chapter Twenty-five

ANXIETY SOUP

I didn't want to hang out in the auditorium after school today, but I'm here anyway, stuck watching Leo rehearse with all of his new friends. It's pouring rain, and my mom said she couldn't pick us up until after work.

So, I'm in the back row, my feet up on the dirty theater seat in front of me. Someone scratched the words *ANYTHING GOES SUX* onto the back of the seat. Leo's onstage with Peregrine, laughing so hard and standing so close. There's no reason for them to be all up against each other, since Daddy Warbucks and Rooster have, like, one scene together, according to Leo.

Peregrine drags Leo to center stage, and, along with the director, they rehearse Leo's big number. I don't even think Peregrine is supposed to be there, but he keeps shouting out pointers to Leo while he performs. It's *so* annoying.

I try to ignore Peregrine, though, because Leo is incredible. He's performing like I've only seen him do in our bedrooms, full-out and with feeling. And in front of everyone in drama club. Actually, he's performing even *better* than he does in our bedrooms. Maybe it's all the rehearsals, but I can't take my eyes off of him. He's a star.

He glances over at Peregrine every few seconds, and then goes back to dancing and singing harder than he was before.

I'm jealous of Peregrine and the other drama club kids that they've been seeing more of Leo than I have, but maybe it's not the worst thing in the world. If we had just stayed as the Al and Leo Club, I wouldn't have to watch this moment where everyone is paying attention to him and seeing him perform. And then maybe *I* wouldn't have started dating Mina because I wouldn't have needed to join the Bathroom Club for something to do.

While my eyes are on Leo, I can't decide if all that's a good or a bad thing.

I try to do some homework, but I wind up messaging with Mina instead.

MINA: can u do that thing where u make ur tongue into a clover??

ME: lol no
i can roll my tongue though

MINA: i can do it
look

She sends a picture of her tongue folded into three sections like a clover. She's in her room, lying on her bed. It's kind of nice to imagine what it would be like if we were both just hanging out there. Maybe if I was even, like, leaning my head against her shoulder or something.

ME: omg ur so talented

MINA: i know 😊

I smile at my phone, then look up to make sure no one's watching me. When I'm texting or FaceTiming Mina, it feels like we're in a separate space where nobody else is allowed. I don't have to worry about people seeing us hanging out in the real world together, or think about *why* I'm so worried that someone might find out.

We can just exist.

That's why I hate it when people say things like, "Oh, you're on your phone too much." I'm really not. That's just where my life is.

Mina tells me she has to help her brother with homework, so I turn my attention back to the stage, where Leo is going over the dance moves for his big number with the person who's playing his sister in the show. They're marking the moves and tripping over each other in a way that makes both of them giggle more than seems necessary.

A thought hits me then, one that I wish would get out

of my brain: If our moms got married, that would make Leo my stepbrother, which would change everything between us.

I mean, things are already different, but still. It would mean that the friendship I have with him would be something more formal; it wouldn't just be the two of us. Even if we were in a fight, we might have to go out to dinner together, or go on a trip with our moms or just . . . exist together, like siblings do. Which I know nothing about since I've been an only child for my entire twelve years of life. I don't know how to be a sibling.

I've tried to keep so many parts of my life as far from each other as possible—Leo, the Bathroom Club, dating Mina, my mom dating Beth—but now it's all blending together and there's nothing I can do to stop it.

I try to get rid of the thoughts by staring into the bright stage lights until my vision turns all yellow. It doesn't work, and I have a giant spot in my vision that makes everything hazy.

Leo finishes performing his song then, and as Peregrine starts to give him notes, I clap a little in my seat.

He must hear me—or at least hear something—because he turns to where I'm sitting, squinting through the same lights I was just staring into. I keep clapping, hoping no one else spots me. Leo smiles and laughs as he waves at me.

I wave back, and, for the second time today, I feel like I'm in my own private world, except this one's with Leo.

Chapter Twenty-six

PRANK GONE WRONG

My mom and Beth are about to leave when Beth turns to us and asks, "You know the number to call in case of an emergency, right?"

It's one of Leo's weekends at home, and I'm ready for a day of the Al and Leo Club, like old times. Especially since our moms will be gone.

"Oh my god Mom, yes, obviously," Leo says, rolling his eyes. "It starts with a nine or something?"

She shakes her head and says, "Just checking, just checking," then comes over and gives Leo one last hug and puts a hand on my shoulder. "Be good today, meyn kinder."

"Beth, we have to go," my mom tells her. She walks over to me like she's going to give me a hug or tell me to only eat raw salmon or something, but then thinks better of it. She pushes her hair back and sighs, walking to the door. "Stay safe," she says.

I nod. It's weird that she didn't even *try* to lecture me, or tell me about all the delicious and nutritious (aka extremely gross) options she left in the fridge for while she was gone. Maybe it's because Beth's here.

"And don't go wrecking the joint, okay?" Beth says.

"We won't," Leo tells her, then he turns to me and stage-whispers, "We will."

Beth and Leo laugh, and my mom nudges Beth out of the door as she waves dramatically to the two of us.

Then they're gone, and it's official: Our moms are going on a *date* (ew).

"So, what do you wanna do?" I ask Leo with a grin once the door is firmly shut. I'm hoping he'll say something like "Hang out and watch Netflix." It's pretty much all I want to do, anyway.

He pinches the flesh between his thumb and index finger. "I kind of . . . invited Peregrine to come over? To rehearse and stuff."

"Oh."

"But you can totally hang out with us if you want! It's just that you might be bored since we're mostly going to be running lines and practicing choreography and stuff like that."

"No, yeah." I grab my phone from the counter so that I have an excuse to turn away from him. I thought this was going to be an Al and Leo day. "I was going to hang out with Mina, so that's perfect." I wasn't, but he doesn't need to know that.

"Cool."

"Yeah."

"I guess I'll see you later, then?" he asks as he opens the door to head back over to his apartment.

"Yeah," I say casually. "Later."

The moment he's in the hallway, I frantically open my texts. Mina hasn't been over to my place yet, mostly because I didn't want her to run into my mom.

But today that's not an issue.

And I *do* want Mina to come over. I want to show her where I live, show her my FaceTime background that she's seen during our late-night conversations and rounds of Among Us. It just sucks that it's only happening because Leo has better things to do.

ME: are u doing anything?

MINA: now?

ME: yea
like do u wanna come over

MINA: this is perfect
i was honestly about to text u to ask if i could come over

ME: wait seriously???

MINA: ya

The fact that she wanted to come over fills my heart up so much that I have to hug my phone to my chest.

MINA: stuff at home is weird now
i need to not be here

I want to be her "not here" place. I like being able to do something for her, help her a little, since she's always the one doing stuff for me. Like explaining colostomy bags and admitting her feelings—you know, chill stuff like that.

So I tell her my address and then clean my room as fast as I possibly can. Even though my bedroom's small, it gets messy really easily. It's like no matter how many T-shirts I pick up off the floor, more respawn out of the T-shirt void.

After a half hour or so, the room is cleaner than it's been in a long time. It's actually kind of cute. When we moved into this apartment, my mom let me order a few things online, like a reversible comforter and a rug shaped like a cloud. And Mina's about to be in here, in the same place as me, not just a voice and a face through my phone. That makes it even better.

It's not like we haven't hung out in person before, but I want this to go so well. I want her to like it here.

So, naturally, my body chooses that moment to send me running to the bathroom.

Peregrine arrives before Mina, which I only know because they're playing music so loudly in Leo's apartment that it's seeping through the walls into mine.

Finally, *my* doorbell rings, and I spring up from my bed, smooth out my hair, check my breath (you never know), and sock slide over the slippery wood floor to the door.

"Hey!" Mina pushes her hair back from her face and grins at me. She's wearing a white T-shirt under a mint-green spaghetti strap dress, which is maybe the best outfit I've ever seen. I scoot away out of the doorway so that she can come in.

"Do you want a snack or something?"

She shakes her head. "I'm good." She's standing next to one of the chairs at the kitchen table, on the verge of sitting down but not quite doing it. She's making me nervous. "So, this is your apartment?"

I nod. "Yup."

"I guess that was kind of a silly question." Mina laughs a little. "I mean, obviously this is your apartment. It's nice, is what I meant to say."

It's really not, but I smile at her anyway.

Across the hall, music's blasting again, and I hear Leo shout, "FIVE, SIX, SEVEN, EIGHT."

"Sorry about that," I tell her. "Leo has a friend over."

Mina raises her eyebrows. "Leo? Like, *Leo* Leo?"

I nod.

"I didn't realize he lived right across the *hall* from you."

She kneels on one of the chairs. "It must be like a sleepover every night!"

My stomach tightens. "Um, kind of." Maybe it used to be like that, but not anymore.

I can't tell Mina about the weirdness going on between me and Leo, though; I can't even figure it out for myself.

We sit in awkward silence, listening to the music blasting through the walls. After a minute, Mina asks, "Should we mess with them?"

"What?"

"Like, we could go over there and scare them," she says. "The music's so loud, they'll never hear us coming."

"I don't know . . ." I thought Mina and I would be hanging out by ourselves. That maybe we'd, like, kiss again or something.

"Please?" she asks, batting her eyelashes dramatically. "It'll be fun."

I take a breath. "All right. Let's do it."

The plan of attack is simple: We sneak into the living room (using the spare key my mom and I have for Beth and Leo's apartment), then tiptoe around the perimeter to Leo's bedroom. There, we'll swing the door open and scream.

It's kind of a basic prank, but scheming with Mina is too fun to point that out. We splayed out on my bedroom floor, and Mina opened her notebook (she takes it everywhere), and had me draw out a "floor plan" of the apartment complex so that we could map our route. We couldn't stop laughing at the mini versions of us she drew off to the side. They looked more like blobs than people.

I try Leo's front door key a few times before I get it to work. "We're in." I whisper it to Mina as the lock clicks open. I say it like I'm a hacker in a movie, which makes her laugh. And then her laughing makes *me* laugh, so we run back into the hallway to get all the giggling out before trying again.

"Ready?" I ask.

She nods. "Roger that."

This time, we're successful. When we're just outside Leo's room, we pause to listen in on what they're doing. The conversation is muffled, so we put our ears to the door.

"You're *so* good at the dance break for 'NYC,'" Leo says.

"Only because you helped me go over it so many times." That's Peregrine.

"Should we run it again?"

"Nooooo," Peregrine whines playfully. "I'm really tired."

"Please? This is my first show," Leo says, and there's a hint of anxiety in his voice. "I want everything to be perfect."

"All right, fine," Peregrine tells him. "But only because you're cute."

I pull my head away from the door and look over at Mina, who raises her eyebrows.

I don't know what I just heard. It could be something

that an eighth grader says to a seventh grader, like, "Oh, you're so cute, like a little kid." But I don't think that's what it was. It sounded like in TV shows when people are trying to, like . . . flirt?

Before I can think about *that* any more, the music starts back up, and Mina nudges my shoulder. She holds up three fingers. "Three," she mouths. "Two." I ready my hand over the door. "One!"

We burst into the room screaming, and Leo practically jumps out of his skin.

When he realizes what's happening, though, he crosses his arms. "Al, what the heck?" He's out of breath, and his eyebrows furrow. "We're in the middle of something."

That's not the reaction I expected. We've pranked each other before, and it always ends with the two of us laughing hysterically—at least after the initial shock is over. "Um . . . okay," I say, crossing my arms too. "You were just being a little loud."

"It has to be loud," he counters. "It's rehearsal."

"It doesn't have to be *that* loud."

But then Mina says, "Hey, Perry," which makes me forget about whatever was going on with Leo.

"Wait, you two know each other?" I ask, looking between Mina and Peregrine.

She nods, biting her lip. "Mhm."

"What? How?" Leo turns to Mina. "Are you also in eighth?"

"She's in seventh," I respond for Mina. "But not at our

school." Which I hope is an obvious enough way to ask how on earth the two of them could possibly know each other. They don't go to the same school. He isn't in the Bathroom Club. So . . . what?

"Oh, yeah." Peregrine shrugs. "We just know each other from this board game night."

"At the Stonewall Center," Mina adds casually. "It's pretty fun."

The Stonewall Center is the queer youth center a few towns over. I've never been, but a representative from there came to our health class one time.

If Peregrine goes to the queer youth center, that must mean he's, well, a queer youth. And if he's queer, then maybe he's picking up on something between me and Mina. Maybe he can just *sense* that we're more than friends. I'm trying to shoot laser beams directly into his skull with my eyes—which, surprise surprise, is not working.

"You two should come to the board game night some-time," Peregrine says, before turning to me and adding, "You know, because of the stuff with your moms."

If Peregrine's saying we should go because of our moms, that means Leo must've told him. And if Leo told him, that means he didn't listen when I said we should never tell anyone about this, ever.

I mean, fine, I told Mina, but only after she pinkie prom-ised on giant tube worms that she wouldn't say anything to anyone until the sun explodes.

"Okay, wait, Perry, we *have* to talk about this," Mina says to Peregrine as if Leo and I aren't here. "Isn't the thing with their moms so cool?"

I have to hold myself back from saying that it's absolutely not.

Peregrine nods, and Leo puts his hands in his pockets.

"I'm literally so jealous," Peregrine says.

"*Same.*"

Leo tries to meet my eye, but no way am I letting him get a look at my irises right now. I don't want to engage our silent Leo and Al communication.

"So, speaking of board games," Leo says a little too loudly, coming to my rescue even if I won't meet his eye. "Do you all wanna play one or something? We have a ton."

I try to silently thank Leo for saving me from a conversation about our moms or anything else, but now *he's* not looking at *me*.

We play a couple rounds of Settlers of Catan (Peregrine wins one and then Mina wins the other), and then Peregrine has to leave for dinner.

"Can I stay a little longer?" Mina asks as we walk back across the hall to my apartment. "I kind of don't want to go home yet."

"Yeah," I tell her. "Of course."

She smiles at me. "Cool." There's a beat of silence. "So, uh, what do you want to do?"

My heart pounds and my stomach churns and the idea

of being alone with Mina is the scariest thing in the world, especially after her talking about how *cool* it is that my mom's dating a woman.

"We can just go to my room and hang out?" I suggest, then realize how that sounds and add, "Like, we could watch TikToks or something."

"Sounds good."

We spend a few minutes watching some vlogs from a YouTuber who also has Crohn's. She has over 100k subscribers even though she mostly talks about IBD, and she's really pretty. Her hair is super curly and short, and she has a septum piercing.

"Would you ever wanna do something like that?" Mina asks when we're done watching one of her videos called *WHAT UR POOP COLOR SAYS ABOUT U!!!!*

"Like what?"

"Make videos about what it's like to have IBD, that kind of thing."

"No," I say quickly. "Definitely not."

I would never want that many people to see my face, let alone hear me talk about poop. I don't mind talking about it in the Bathroom Club group chat, but I have my limits.

"I think I'd like to do something like that," Mina says.

"You'd be really good at it." She's so confident when she's talking about her colostomy bag, and, well, everything.

"I'd want you to be in the videos too, though," she says. "Like, we could do a girlfriend tag or something like that."

I look down. "Yeah," I tell her. "Maybe."

"Or not, if you wouldn't want to," she adds quickly. "I was just saying, like, it would be cool. It's not real, obviously."

"I just don't like being in front of a camera that much."

"Oh." She scooches a little so our legs aren't touching anymore. "But you do still want to be my girlfriend, right?"

I nod. "Yes!" Then, slightly quieter: "Yes."

It's just that I don't want anyone to know.

It's not that I'm ashamed of her, it's more that I'm ashamed of myself. It's mortifying just to be alive and have a body. For people to look at me and see a human being who has poop and feelings.

I move my leg back so that it's touching hers again. She smiles shyly and reaches out her pinkie. I wrap mine around hers, and we sit like that for a second.

Girlfriends in private.

Chapter Twenty-seven

PIZZA-LESS IN THE AUDITORIUM

I don't know how I got roped into doing stage crew. I really thought it would be something that I told Rikako I would do, and then they'd never follow up on it.

But they texted me last night and told me they "expected to see me there bright and early!" It sounded nice, but I knew they were being serious.

I don't want to see Leo and Peregrine hanging out and being best friends all morning, but it's set-painting day. Rikako was expecting me, so here I am, spending a Sunday at school.

It's just that Leo's been my number one person since sixth grade. It's hard to see him be as seemingly close with someone else.

"Okay, red team needs to go paint the NYC backdrop," Rikako shouts into the auditorium. She's super organized and has us split up into four teams so that we always know what our assignment is.

The one good thing is that Carl got roped into set painting too, and he's in my group.

Carl and I head over to the canvas backdrop that's laid across the stage floor, grab some old paintbrushes, and get to work. It's pretty relaxing to paint the sets. It's like color-by-number, since everything is laid out for us. Red goes here, blue goes there, and I just dip the brush in the paint and go to town. But of course the actors wouldn't know that, because they're barely painting even though that's their job for today too. They're too busy singing and running choreography and generally screaming at the top of their lungs.

"Do you think they know how loud they are?" Carl whispers. Our heads are close together as we paint the streetlights on the backdrop.

"Absolutely not," I tell him, and we both giggle.

We turn to watch the big group, and of course Leo and Peregrine are at the center of it. I haven't seen Leo interacting with drama club people a ton outside of rehearsal, but they all seem to love him (obviously). He's doing some dance move where he swings his arms in a circle, and the people are eating it up. He's making them laugh in a way he only ever used to do for me. There are a few tiny sixth-grade girls gathered around him, fluttering like humming-birds by a flower.

I stop staring at Leo and get back to work on the set. The more I focus on him, the more my stomach gurgles. It's taking away from the relaxing activity of accidentally splattering paint all over myself while helping with sets.

"How's it going over here?" Rikako asks us after a few minutes.

"Good," Carl tells her. He's painting neater lines than me, with his knees tucked under him, bent forward at the waist. I feel so comfortable around Carl, maybe because he's good at explaining things to me, like how to properly hold a paintbrush or the plots of old movies and things like that.

"Carl," Rikako starts, and he looks up. "Would you mind helping the green group with their section? I think they need someone who actually knows how to draw *inside the lines*." She yells that part over to the group near us, and most of them roll their eyes.

When Carl is out of earshot, Rikako sits next to me with a big sigh. Their leggings are ripped and covered in all different colors of paint, but in a cool artsy way. It makes them look even more like the official stage manager they are.

She nods in Leo's direction. "The cast really likes him."

"Cool." I shouldn't be annoyed that everyone loves Leo, but I am. He's *my* . . . Leo.

They pick up a paintbrush to help me out with this section of the set. "So, you liking crew? You think you'll work on the summer stock show?" Rikako asks, but before I can answer, she says, "I was thinking of asking Mina to do stage crew for that show too, since it's not through the school or anything."

I shrug, like this is super casual news. "Maybe I'd think about it, then."

She nudges my knee with hers and grins. "I bet she wouldn't mind working late nights backstage with you . . ."

I look around to make sure no one's listening in, then lower my voice. "What are you talking about?"

They smile and lower their voice too. "You're cute together. I feel like she definitely has a crush on you."

"How do you know?" I hold my breath waiting for an answer, my stomach clenching.

"It's just a vibe." They shrug. "I'm bi, so I can usually tell things like that."

My stomach's just about ready to burst through my skin and out onto the auditorium floor. "You are?"

"I feel like I've definitely mentioned this," Rikako says, laughing a little. "I talk about it, like, all the time."

Uh, they definitely have *not* mentioned it. If they had, I would've remembered.

But now that Rikako's figured out there's something going on between me and Mina, maybe I should tell her. She'd be the first person I've ever told, even if she's already figured it out.

I try to calm my aching stomach, but it's like a tsunami in there. After a few seconds, I make up my mind.

I lean close to them and whisper, "We're dating," so quietly that *I* can barely hear it.

Rikako leans in closer. "What?"

"We're kind of, like, dating," I say, slightly louder but still at a whisper. "Me and Mina."

Rikako covers their mouth with a hand. "That's so cute, OMG."

"Shhhh," I tell her, but I'm smiling a little. It honestly *is* cute. And I'm glad Rikako agrees, because they're the only other person I know—aside from Mina—who's queer *and* has Crohn's, and seems to be handling it pretty well, all things considered. They even have enough energy to be the stage manager.

She laughs a little, then whispers, "Poor Carl's going to be a fifth wheel."

"I know," I say. "I feel so bad."

"He'll be fine," Rikako says quietly as we avoid looking over at him. "He's always told the group that he never wants to date anyone. And it's not like you stop being friends with other people when you start dating someone."

"That's good, then," I say. "So we'll still just hang out, the five of us, right? As the Bathroom Club?"

"Of course," they say. "Bathroom Club for life."

The rest of the morning passes in a blur of painting sets and eating the plainest doughnuts.

"And that's a wrap," Rikako shouts into the auditorium as the sun is going down. "And as a little treat . . ." She gives a thumbs-up to the back of the auditorium, and some of the show parents bring out a bunch of boxes of pizza.

Everyone cheers, but I hang back. Pizza will *not* sit well with my stomach. Apparently, it won't sit well with Carl's, either, because he stays with me and says, "This was fun. I'm glad Rikako made us both do stage crew."

"I'm glad too," I say, even if that's not the whole truth. "How come she didn't force Ethan to help paint sets?"

Carl shrugs. "I don't think kids from other schools are allowed to help with drama club."

"His loss," I say, trying to seem cheerful in front of Carl. "He didn't get hot chocolate."

Carl and I say goodbye after that and he wanders over to Rikako. Then I'm alone, pizza-less in the auditorium.

"Hey!" Leo walks up to me, balancing a slice of pizza on a paper plate.

"Hey," I say, arms crossed.

"How'd it go?" He rips off a piece of the crust and eats it. "Sorry that the actors had to leave early to work on some blocking. It's just, you know, tech week." He shrugs his shoulders and keeps eating.

"I guess." Then, after a minute: "It seems like you've got a little fan club or something."

The way the girls gathered around him was like a punch in my already-hurting gut.

He smiles awkwardly. "I wouldn't call it a fan club."

"All those sixth-grade girls seem to think you're cool."

"Maybe," he says. "It's just nice to have other people who are also in a show for the first time."

Then I feel bad for saying anything, because of course Leo's nervous and he wants to hang out with people who understand what he's going through.

When he's done with his pizza, Leo says an extended goodbye to every single actor in the cast—with an even *more* extended goodbye for Peregrine—as I wait by the auditorium doors. It makes me think about how we haven't done our secret handshake in ages. I wonder if he even remembers it.

When he's done, we walk out to the parking lot and sit on the steps leading up to the front entrance of the school. Leo folds himself over and rests his cheek on the top of his knees, facing me. "So what were you and Rikako talking about in there?"

Oh, no.

Did Leo overhear? What if he's just asking because he wants me to tell him?

"I thought you were too busy hanging out with your actor friends to notice." I know it's rude, but at least it takes the focus off me.

"I was still keeping tabs on you."

I roll my eyes. "I don't need you to keep tabs on me. I'm literally fine."

He puts his hands up. "Okay, okay."

We sit in silence until our moms come to pick us up. I run into the car so that no one sees the four of us together, but Leo takes his sweet time.

"Who's ready for some dinner?" Beth asks once we're home. "I made pizza!"

"They just gave us pizza at set painting," I tell her.

"So?" Leo looks over at me. "That was just an appetizer. This will be main-course pizza."

Beth laughs. "I love the idea of appetizer pizza and main-course pizza. Maybe we could even have dessert pizza too.

I think I have some Nutella and marshmallows in the pantry, and I could whip up a quick dough."

No one objects to that, even though all I want to do is fall into bed and FaceTime Mina. I can't, though, because this is a "group dinner."

Once we're done with the meal, Beth's dessert pizza is ready. It's so sweet that I can barely have a bite before I start feeling nauseous.

When my mom and I get ready to leave, Beth pulls me aside, out of earshot of my mom and Leo.

"I just wanted to check in with you, if that's okay," she says.

I just cross my arms, but she must take that as a sign that it *is* okay, when really, it's a sign that if I try to say anything I might scream at the top of my lungs.

"I want to make sure that you're feeling all right with all of this." She gestures around her apartment as if she was talking about our dinner and not about her being my mom's girlfriend. "I know it's a big adjustment for you and Leo, but I hope you'll remember that I'm *always* here to talk."

"Okay," I say. I stare at the door to make it clear that I want to leave.

"Do you have any questions?" she asks. "I'm happy to answer anything and everything. Leo and I have talked about it, so I want to make sure you're doing all right too."

I nod and say, "Cool," even though I don't know what I'm "cool"ing. She doesn't have to remind me that she's talked to Leo about all this when my mom and I haven't touched the subject with a million-foot pole.

I don't want to be rude, but I need to go back to my room, and also probably sit on the toilet for like three hours. "May I be excused?" I ask quietly. It's the most formal I've ever been with Beth.

"Of course, bubs," she says, and I run to my room, where I can text Mina in private.

Chapter Twenty-eight

TIME TO FLUSH MY PHONE DOWN THE TOILET

Beth created a group chat and named it "2nd-Floor Bubs," because me, my mom, Beth, and Leo all live on the second floor of the apartment complex. And apparently now we need a group chat, because we have so much to coordinate.

> BETH: Family Dinner tonight!
> I'm making something special.

> LEO: is it brisket
> plz

> BETH: 😮 I'll never tell
> JK, it is Brisket!

It's hard not to cringe at Beth's overly formal texting style, and even harder not to cringe at the idea of all of us having dinner again, especially after the way things went the other night when Beth tried to get us to bond over two types of pizza.

My mom's still finishing up a shift at the grocery store, so she doesn't respond.

I don't have an excuse, but I don't respond either.

Mina texts me right after Beth's message comes in, which could be luck or could just be the fact that we text, like, all the time.

MINA: hey um i know this is kind of last minute but can i come over to ur house

ME: wait rn??

MINA: if that's ok???
my dad's here and he's fighting with my mom
and my brothers at a sleepover
and i just cant deal w this

ME: i want u to!!
but we're having a family dinner tn so idk if u can

MINA: u and ur mom?

ME: no me and my mom and
leo and his mom

MINA: WAIT NOW I SUPER HAVE TO COME
i wanna see what ur mom and leo's mom are like
~together~

I squeeze my eyes shut. I personally *don't* want her to see what my mom and Beth are like, because it won't be anything good, but I tell her I'll ask Beth.

Hopefully she'll say no.

Instead of texting in the group chat to check in with Beth, I walk down to the bakery, where she's wiping the counters.

"Hey," I say, waving awkwardly as I lean against the glass pastry case.

"Hey bubs." She doesn't look up from her wiping.

"I was wondering if it would be okay for one of my friends from my support group to come to our dinner?" I realize after I ask it how much it sounds like I'm asking a parent's permission for something, even though Beth is *not* my mom. I also feel bad for calling Mina my friend, but I can't call her anything else to Beth. "It's *really* okay if she can't, I told her we were having like a fancy dinner and stuff."

Beth grins. "No way, bring her! The more the merrier. I already cooked enough to feed everyone in town, so one more can't hurt."

And there goes my excuse. Beth wants my "friend" from support group to come. This should be fun—a dinner with my mom and her girlfriend and my secret girlfriend and my best friend who I barely know anymore because he spends all his time with drama club people.

A super normal evening.

• • •

Okay fine, I was wrong, it actually *is* fun.

Mina is her usual talkative self, and she has my mom and Beth laughing at every other word she says. She talks about her old hamster and how her brother let it out into the snow and then six months later it came back, too thin but still alive. She talks about how nice it's been to get to know me at support group (that one makes me blush).

Leo catches my eye and motions to his phone under the table, and I pull my phone out from under my leg to check it.

LEO: what's up w mina?

ME: what do u mean??

I look up, and he shrugs.

LEO: like why is she here??

ME: shes my friend??

LEO: ok . . .

I roll my eyes and shove my phone back between my thigh and the chair. Then Mina knocks her knee into mine under the table, and I'm brought back to my non-phone world with a pang in my stomach from Mina's touch. Even with my mom and Leo and Beth around, it's like our own private conversation, only it's knee-to-knee communication.

When my mom and Beth aren't looking, Mina mouths "I love them," and it feels like our private world is done. I pull my knee away.

"How are we feeling about dessert?" Beth asks as she pushes her chair back from the table.

"Amazing," Mina says excitedly. "I *love* your biscochos, Ms. Klein."

Beth holds her hand to her chest. "Oh my goodness, bubala, that's so sweet." She pads over to the kitchen and opens the oven, grinning. "And you're in luck, because I've got a fresh batch ready to go!"

Mina gasps like she just won the lottery. Even Leo smiles.

Beth carries the tray over and plops it down in front of us on the table. The cookies are small and round, shaped like tiny bagels and covered in sesame seeds.

"Are you sure that's a good idea, Al?" my mom asks. "I don't think you're supposed to have seeds."

"Well, lucky for you I made some without sesame seeds!" Beth says quickly, grabbing another tray out of the oven. "I thought it would be helpful to have the option—and for you too, Mina!"

"Thanks," Mina says, and grabs one of the non-seeded ones.

I grab one covered in sesame seeds. My mom sighs.

"These are *so* good," Mina says after a minute of happy chewing.

"Agreed, honey, these are perfect," my mom says, rubbing her hand in circles on Beth's back.

I want to run directly to the bathroom, but Mina brightens even more.

"So," Mina says, leaning forward in her chair and speaking to my mom and Beth, who are giving each other the grossest love-y eyes. "How did you two, like, start dating?"

I dig my fingernails into my palm, fighting the urge to snap at Mina. Of course this is something she wants to know. She even *told* me she thought it was cool that my mom has a girlfriend.

And, even though part of me wants to run away, another part kind of wants to know the answer. It's not like my mom and I would ever talk about it. This might be my only chance.

Beth and my mom share a glance, then Beth sighs happily and leans forward. "Well, bubs, the thing is, we were friends first," she says. She looks between Mina and me, speaking cautiously. "We loved spending time together, and it just . . ." Beth shrugs. "Turned into something more."

I stare down at my lap so that no one can see that my face is about to burn off.

"That's *so* sweet," Mina says while grabbing another biscocho. "That's just like how Al and I—"

"Became better friends," I say, cutting her off. "We're really good friends now."

Beth nods, though she's clearly confused. "I'm so glad to hear it, bubs."

I can't look up, but I can *feel* everyone's eyes on me. The hairs on the back of my neck are prickling, and my stomach is sloshing, a moment away from total disaster. If I let Mina tell everyone that we're dating, everything would come crashing down. I wouldn't have anything left to call my own.

I can feel the way Mina's body has shifted away from me. I know I shouldn't have said that, but I didn't know what else to do.

The only sound for the next few minutes is all of us eating biscochos.

"I think my mom's actually here to pick me up," Mina says finally, without her usual enthusiasm. "But thank you so much for having me."

I know that's a lie. Her mom didn't even drop her off. She lives close enough to walk, and there are well-lit sidewalks the whole way. The idea of her running away like this makes me want to cry.

"You're welcome, bubs," Beth says, grabbing everyone's plates and piling more biscochos onto them.

Once Mina's gone, Beth points to the door she just ran out of. "She seems nice!"

"Yup," I tell her.

When I head back to my room, there are no texts from Mina waiting for me. Not that I expected any.

Except maybe I did. Ever since we exchanged numbers, we've texted every day. I try to scroll back to our earlier messages, but it takes forever because we've been talking so much.

And now I'm going to lose all of that. Maybe that's what has to happen, though, because the alternative of my mom and Beth and Leo finding out about me dating Mina at dinner would've been horrible. And scary. And *weird*.

I want to message her that I'm sorry, that I couldn't have her telling my mom and Beth and Leo that we're dating, but it's too much to explain.

Instead, I watch TikToks from my main account of kids from my school dancing badly, as a punishment for myself.

But an hour later, all I want to do is talk to Mina. Even though I tried to make it seem like we were just friends at dinner. She's my girlfriend, after all. Well, I hope she still is.

So I send her a picture of a tube worm, hoping it'll be enough.

She thumbs-up reacts to the photo. That's it. Not even a heart. Maybe I don't deserve a heart.

ME: do u think maybe we could facetime?

MINA: i'd rather not

I hate reading that text knowing that I'm the reason she's responding like that.

It's just that I want to be able to see her face while we're talking; I can't tell how she's feeling from her texts.

I go back to TikTok, but after a minute, *she* FaceTimes *me*. I don't know what made her change her mind.

"Hey," I say, sitting down on my bed, excited to see her face on my phone even though she looks more miserable than I've ever seen her.

"Hey," she says, her voice too even. "What did you want to talk about?"

"It's whatever," I tell her, looking down at the rug.

"I mean, it's clearly not," she says.

She's right, but I don't know how to tell her what I really want to say. That she's made having Crohn's feel like something good rather than the tragedy I initially thought it would be. That I love to hear her talk about tube worms and large rodents and anything and everything.

But that I also don't want other people to know about us. Especially not my mom.

"I just, like, wanted to see if you were okay after ... what happened."

"What happened, Al?" she asks, sounding more upset than I've ever heard her. "Like, do your mom and Beth even know that we're dating?"

I shake my head, avoiding Mina's eyes on my phone.

"They're dating *each other*." Mina says it like she's

explaining the alphabet to a kindergartener. "They wouldn't care that you're dating a girl."

"But *I* do," I say before I can even think about how it sounds.

Because it's true. It's so, so scary, to have someone who's *yours*, who you're supposed to kiss and hug. Who you're supposed to let know everything about you, which is almost impossible when you don't know *anything* and you're embarrassed to just be yourself.

When I look up, Mina's crying, and I want to take it all back.

"You know that the Bathroom Club knows I'm queer, right?" she asks. "I told them last year that I'm a lesbian. I like that I don't have to hide who I am."

"Oh," I say, feeling worse about myself than I ever have. "I didn't know."

She shrugs, like she couldn't care less. "So, do you not want to be dating?" she asks finally. "If you care so much about your mom not knowing?"

I shrug. "I don't know."

And I really don't. I like Mina so much, but I'm just not ready to be as open as she is. I don't know if I ever will be.

"Do you think we should go back to being just friends?" she asks. "And only see each other at support group and stuff?"

My stomach is gurgling so loud, I'm sure Mina can hear it, but she doesn't say anything.

"Yeah, I guess so," I tell her, even though I *don't* think we'd be better as friends. Even though she's the prettiest, nicest, smartest person I've ever met in my life and I want to keep kissing her and hanging out with her and learning more about her.

"Okay." Her face hardens. "Yeah."

"Mina, I'm sorry," I start, and I can tell she's about to say something when I add, "But I have to go to the bathroom."

I hang up and run to the toilet and for once in my life I'm not pooping at all. I'm sobbing.

I never should've said anything. I never should've texted her. It would've been better for both of us if I had deleted her number and then flushed my phone down the toilet for good measure. The fish can have it.

Chapter Twenty-nine

FIGHTING IN THE GROCERY STORE

I'm glad this is one of Leo's weekends at his dad's house, because I don't want to hang out with him; I want to stay in bed and mope.

Which involves: staring at the ceiling, then lying on my stomach, then groaning a lot.

I would mope in other parts of the apartment, but I've been avoiding my mom. I *could* say that our schedules haven't intersected, but that's not true. It's more that I don't want to be in the same place as her, especially since that dinner.

"Can you come with me to grab a few things from the grocery store?" my mom asks, popping her head into my room.

"Can't I just stay in the apartment?"

"You could," she says. "But I feel like we haven't had any Mom and Al time in a while. And we can get Starbucks."

My heart drops into my stomach. So, she's noticed too.

I roll my eyes and grab my jacket. "Fine." My mom knows that getting a really sweet pink iced tea with extra lemon at the Starbucks next to the grocery store is one of my favorite things to do, and I can't say no to a giant iced tea.

I keep my arms crossed as we walk out to the car, but when we're in there, something changes. With the outside world muffled, it's sort of like we're in our own little bubble. My mom and I both relax.

"How has the support group been?" she asks as she pulls out of her parking spot.

"Fine," I tell her. Then the car-bubble-magic does its work and I add, "It feels like I can be myself around everyone in the group. Because they all know what it's like to have a chronic illness too."

"That's great." She takes a breath. "And Mina's a good friend now?" She looks over at me quickly. "It was nice meeting her the other night. She seems lovely."

My stomach goes into overdrive. "Yeah," I say. "I guess."

After that I can feel myself twisting away from my mom, closing off.

We pull into one of the employee spots in the grocery store parking lot, and I put my hood up. I used to like going to the grocery store with her, back when she would sneak me free samples and push me too fast in a shopping cart. Now I lag a few steps behind her the whole time while she greets her coworkers and grabs some apples from the produce section.

"Can we just get Starbucks now?" I whisper after a few minutes.

"We'll get it when I'm done."

My mom throws sliced turkey and bread into the cart, and I do everything I can not to pout, especially when I get a snap from Leo showing the huge congratulatory spread his dad got him for the show tomorrow. It has all of Leo's favorite Filipino snacks and some pastries and Jewish desserts from the bakery that Beth must've contributed.

I hold up the turkey in the cart and mumble, "Do we *have* to eat this for, like, every meal?"

"I thought you liked turkey?" my mom asks, distracted by the nutrition facts on the back of a can of pinto beans. "Plus, it's easy on the stomach."

I throw the package of sliced meat back into the cart harder than I probably should.

"Al," my mom warns.

I roll my eyes, but my vision blurs with tears.

"I'm gonna wait in the car," I say, and run out into the parking lot. It's a maze of people with shopping carts and giant bags, and I'm out of breath by the time I reach our car. It's locked, so I just lean against it.

"What's going on?" my mom asks when she finally comes outside, a reusable bag in hand. She smooths her hair out and unlocks the door. "Get in."

She walks around to the driver's side and I sit in the passenger seat and slam the door. It's only a short drive, and I don't want to add insult to injury by being a baby and sitting in the back.

"What happened?" she asks, and it comes out more gently than when we were outside of the car. "Why'd you run out like that?"

I shrug and grunt out the universal *I don't know* sound.

"Is everything okay at school?"

I turn to glare at her, then go back to staring out of the window. I hate that that's her first thought. That she doesn't even realize it might be something at *home* that's bothering me, not school.

"Yup."

"Is it something else, then?" she asks. "You've been acting differently lately."

Maybe that's because I finally found a group of people who have the same chronic illness as me and don't try to stop me from eating or doing what I want.

"Okay . . ."

She shakes her head. "You need to give me more than that."

I really don't think I do. But after a minute I say, "It's not school."

She nods. "All right." She takes a breath. "Okay."

I glance over at her, and there are tears streaming out of her eyes.

The next breath she takes is shaky and phlegmy. "Is it me, then?" she asks. "Are you . . . are you ashamed of me or something?"

She's really crying now, and I am too.

It's so unfair: It's unfair to ask me that. It's unfair to have a kid when all you do is worry about them.

"Can you say *something*?" she asks after a minute of us both crying harder than we ever have in front of each other.

I don't want to, but I take a breath. Seeing my mom cry cracks something open inside of me. I have plenty to say.

"You just . . . You make my life so hard," I tell her through sobs. "Like, I don't want to eat turkey every night because you think it's the only thing that I can handle. I don't even *like* turkey." I sniffle and continue. "I want you to just be there for me, and not ask me 'Oh, are you sure you want to eat that?' every time I'm about to eat *anything*. I don't want you to always be worrying about me, because it makes me feel *horrible* about myself."

My mom clears her throat, but I can't look at her, because if I do, I don't think I'll be able to say the rest.

"Everything's already so hard." I bend over and sob into my thighs, and say the next part hoping she can't hear, because I know before I say it that it's not fair. "I'm already the kid with Crohn's, and now I have to be the kid with a queer mom who's dating my best friend's mom. My life is so much harder now that you're dating Beth."

I can barely catch my breath now, and I still can't look up at my mom. I just said one of the worst things I've ever told any human being. Even if most of it is true, I'm worried she hates me.

"Can we please just go home?" I ask through tears, my head still between my legs, staring at the dirty passenger seat floor.

She doesn't say anything, but she turns the car on.

"Sit up," she tells me, her voice thick with tears but pretty much emotionless. "Your head will snap off if we get into a crash."

I don't say anything, but I follow her command and sit up and face the window.

We don't talk for the whole drive, and when we're back in the apartment, we both go straight to our rooms. I can hear her crying through the door.

Chapter Thirty

I'M NEVER DANCING AGAIN

Here's a list of all the things I did last night:

Cry

Poop

That's it.

It's now Sunday, the day of Leo's show, but that's not till later.

The last thing I want is to talk to *anyone*, but Ethan sends a message to the Bathroom Club group chat, and I can't stop myself from opening it while I'm on the toilet.

ETHAN: send me ur location rn

CARL: creepy
lskjsl
sorry that was anchovy
he stepped on my ipad

RIKAKO: hi chovy!
and ethan u know where i am

CARL: ok that's even creepier

MINA: why??

ETHAN: we're going to the greatest place on earth

CARL: disney?

ETHAN: no lol
how would we even get there?

CARL: idk!!!!!!! just guessing

ETHAN: no we're going to . . .
BOUNCE!!!
my mom's taking us there
her treat dw
im calling an emergency meeting

CARL: :0 v mysterious

ETHAN: what can I say?

Even with everything going on, I have to laugh. Because Ethan is trying to get us to have a meeting at an indoor trampoline park.

ME: i have leo's show later

That's mostly an excuse, because at this point, I just want to hide in my bedroom forever.

RIKAKO: so do i lol
AND i'm the stage manager
but there's so much time bc the actors are doing "just actors" bonding stuff

ETHAN: i'll pick everyone up i promise

I don't really want to go, but I also don't want to stay in my apartment with my mom. I can either be miserable here, or be miserable at Bounce with my friends (and kind-of ex-girlfriend).

So, Bounce it is.

"I now call this emergency meeting of the Bathroom Club to order," Ethan says as we all stand in a circle on the giant trampoline.

After a minute, one of the employees calls out to us and says, "YOU GOTTA BOUNCE. BOUNCE OR YOU'RE DONE."

So, we all start bouncing. Rikako jumps the highest, but I just hop a bit. I don't think my stomach can take a full bounce. Mina's not bouncing at all, and I'm trying not to look over at her. (And failing.)

Even though I can feel the Bounce employee giving me the stink eye, I can't bring myself to bounce any more than I already am. My stomach hurts too much from all the stuff going on: First, everything went wrong with Mina, and then everything went wrong with my mom.

To top it all off, my mom doesn't exactly know where I am right now. I mean, I said "I'm leaving" when I ran out of the apartment. But she was in her room and I said it super quietly, so I doubt she heard me. And then I got the kind of stomach pain that only happens when I know I did something really, really bad.

"How is this an emergency meeting if there's no emergency?" Mina asks, staring down at the trampoline floor.

"Yeah," Carl says, losing his balance after a big jump. "Honestly, it just seems like an excuse to get us all to go to the trampoline place."

"Oh, it definitely is," Rikako says. "He's been telling me he wants to go here forever."

"All right, all right." Ethan bends his knees to stop the bouncing, but then the employee points at him, so he starts back up again. "It's not an emergency. I just wanted to hang out—fine, there, I said it."

Carl crosses his arms mid-bounce. "You could've told us that."

"Yeah, but isn't it more fun to say it's an emergency?" Ethan asks.

"I thought you were having a flare-up or something!"

Carl jumps toward Ethan and tries to tackle him, but the force of the bounce causes both of them to land on their butts.

"Can we not fight about this?" Mina sort of mumbles to her mismatched-socked feet.

"We're not fighting," Ethan says. He bounces as high as he can, gaining momentum and then doing a flip. His mom cheers from her spot on the non-trampoline ground.

"Is all this bouncing making anyone else's stomach mad?" Carl asks after a minute.

"Oh, definitely me," I tell him. I'm on the verge of pooping my pants, but at the same time, there's something about a trampoline floor that's knocking the bad feelings out of me. It's like the more I bounce, the better I feel. I like the repetitive motion, how easy it is to jump and jump and jump.

"Eh, it's fine," Rikako says. Although she doesn't *look* fine, if you know what I mean. "Just keep bouncing. I have to leave soon anyway."

"I thought Aneliza said to listen to our stomachs," Carl says.

"Sometimes our stomachs lie to us," Rikako says, then bounces super high and does a toe-touch midair, stretching their arms all the way to the tips of their feet.

"Wait, I wanna try that," Mina says as she gets ready to jump. She gets the momentum, but then she's too high in the air and she tries to twist her body into a toe-touch and lands on her butt.

After a moment, she bursts out in a fit of giggles, and Carl hops over to help her up.

"THIS IS YOUR SECOND WARNING," the employee shouts. "BOUNCE NOW."

This only makes all of us laugh harder, because how is Mina supposed to bounce when she just landed on her butt *from* a bounce?

I let the others help Mina up—I doubt she wants me grabbing her hand right now—but once she's back to bouncing I say, "Let's all try to jump at the same time. Then we could do a super bounce."

"YEAH!" Ethan shouts, half running and half jumping across the trampoline.

Everyone stands in a circle and stops jumping.

"All right, on the count of three," I say.

I glance around the circle at Ethan and Rikako and Carl and, finally, Mina. They all give me a nod.

"One." I crouch down. "Two." Here we go. "Three!"

We all spring up at the same time, and when we come back down and bounce again, the force of all of our feet on the trampoline at once sends us springing back up, so high that we lose control.

I bump into Carl, who bumps into Ethan, who grabs on to Rikako, whose elbow smacks into Mina's stomach.

But when we fall down, landing in a pile of limbs and sweat and laughter, all I want to do is lie down here with these people forever.

Until: "THAT'S STRIKE THREE. I LITERALLY COULD

NOT HAVE BEEN ANY CLEARER. YOU HAVE TO BOUNCE."

So, we make our way off of the trampoline, giggling together.

Even if two of us just broke up. Even if it feels like the end of the world.

It's still the five of us.

The Bathroom Club.

"All right, now we can really get down to business," Ethan says as we sit in his basement an hour or so later. He invited us all back to his house, but only me and Carl came. Rikako had to go to the school to help set up for the show, and Mina just . . . left.

It's only like four in the afternoon now, though, and the show doesn't start till much later, so I decided to come. The bigger problem is that my mom still has no idea where I am, but I can't bring myself to worry about that right now. She most likely hasn't even realized that I'm gone. I bet she's still in her room, and she thinks I'm still in mine.

"Was Mina acting kind of weird?" Ethan asks, grabbing a handful of chips from the coffee table.

"Yeah, is she okay?" Carl asks.

They both look over at me.

"Why are you asking *me*?"

"Because you two are so close." Ethan doesn't say it like

he knows we were dating, which I'm happy about, because it means that Rikako hasn't told him. Not that I thought they would, but still.

I shrug. "We got into a fight."

"Well, that explains it," Carl says, sitting on his heels on the couch. "What happened?"

My shoulders find their way into a shrug yet again. "Nothing."

"You sure?" Ethan asks. "Mina is never this upset."

"Dude, don't say *that*," Carl tells him.

"But it's true."

Carl shakes his head at Ethan, but then I take a deep breath and say, "You're right," and they turn to look at me.

"It's way bigger than just a fight with Mina," I admit, and just saying that feels good. It feels honest about everything that's been going on.

"I knew it," Carl says.

"I personally don't know anything," Ethan adds, and we all laugh, even Ethan.

"Okay, so, can I tell you two something?" I ask, and they both nod. "It's not a bad thing or anything. It's just that I'm queer. I like girls, mostly."

Carl grins. "Oh, cool," he says. "I'm aromantic, so, like, I get it."

I turn to him. "Wait, really?"

"Yeah, I was trying to find a way to tell you two, actually. I mean, Rikako and Mina know, and maybe you could tell?"

He smiles. "It was never a secret, but it's cool that there are a bunch of us who are queer in the group."

"This is *amazing*," I say. "It's like . . . beshert." It's Yiddish for "meant to be."

"Totally," Ethan says, then turns to me, his eyes on the floor. "And actually . . ."

"Dude, you too?" Carl asks, grinning.

"Yup." Ethan nods. "I think I might be queer too. I mean, I don't really know, but I think some boys are cute, or whatever. And sometimes I don't even know if I'm fully a boy. But *he/him* pronouns are still good."

"This is so cool," Carl says.

"Agreed," I say.

I might not have told them everything, but even just the part that I did get off my chest feels incredible.

And then I start laughing. I laugh so hard that I can't stop. That it's hurting my stomach. "Wait, are we all queer?"

"I mean, I know Mina is," Carl says, laughing a little too. "She talks about it all the time."

Even the mention of Mina doesn't make me stop laughing. "How come we didn't talk about this sooner? It's like we're an IBD support group *and* an LGBTQ club."

Maybe part of the reason we all got along so well in the first place is because we subconsciously knew that we were all queer.

"We should do something," Ethan says suddenly.

"Are you thinking what I'm thinking?" Carl asks.

Ethan grins and grabs one of his Switch remotes. "Shall we dance?"

"What?" I ask, but Carl's already giggling.

"Don't make her do that."

"Well, you don't have to, obviously," Ethan says, turning to me. "But if you wanted to, I have Just Dance on my Switch and, I don't know. Sometimes it helps to put all your feelings into *dance*."

"It's what Ethan and I do when we hang out," Carl says. "You can be part of it too, though."

I smile at him, and Carl nods encouragingly. I've never hung out alone with Carl and Ethan, but I *do* kind of want to dance out my feelings if it means not talking about Mina and my mom.

Ethan navigates over to Just Dance and picks a song. "Carl and I can show you how it's done, and then you can take a turn."

"Sounds good," I tell him, and before I know it, a Dua Lipa song is blaring from the TV.

I expect them to just use their arms, to struggle with following along with the people on the screen, but I couldn't be more wrong. They know all of the choreography, and they're jumping around, swinging their hips and hitting every move perfectly.

When they're done, they collapse back on the couch, and I clap for them. "That was so good."

"What can I say?" Ethan pants. "We're pros."

"We got the highest score in the world on that song one day." Carl grabs a pretzel from the table, looking proud of himself, as he should.

Ethan hands me one of the controllers. "Wanna give it a try?"

I nod, but I don't move. "Can you do it with me?"

Ethan nods and starts scrolling through song options. "This is the easiest one," he tells me as he picks one from the kids' section. It's called "Get on the Fire Truck" and the people dancing on the screen are dressed as firefighters.

"Ready?" Ethan asks.

"No," I tell him honestly. My stomach cramps up just as the song starts, and even though Carl is the only person in the audience, I'm nervous.

It's embarrassing at first, especially because the people on the screen are so good at dancing, but after a minute I get a few "perfects" on the moves and Ethan and Carl are cheering me on and I start to lose myself in the very silly song.

When it's over, I'm sweaty, but I'm not nervous at all anymore. "Can we do more?"

"Definitely," Ethan says, and we all take turns dancing and bouncing around and screaming the songs at the top of our lungs.

It's amazing.

I lose track of how long we play for, but after a long while I grab my jacket from the corner of the room to check my phone.

And I have thirty-four texts and five missed calls.

From Leo. And my mom. And Beth.

"Wait, it's seven thirty?" I ask. My stomach clenches and my hands start sweating.

How did it get so late? How did I not check the time?

Oh no.

"I guess so," Ethan says, stretching his hands over his head. "You can stay for dinner if you want."

"No, my—" I almost say "my brother." Almost. "The show is happening right now. Like, the one Rikako was working on."

"She said we didn't have to go to that," Carl says. "Since she's just working backstage and we wouldn't even see her except during the set changes."

"Yeah, but my friend is in it, and I promised him I would go." I'm panicking now. It started half an hour ago, and I have no way of getting there since Beth is already at the show and I definitely can't call my mom.

According to my phone, it would take thirty minutes to walk to school from Ethan's, so I don't walk.

I run.

I run so fast that even Mr. DiMeglio would be impressed.

By the time I get to the school, I'm shaking and I have to poop so badly that I might not make it to a bathroom.

But I do, and then I sneak into the back of the auditorium.

The kids in the ensemble have their hands clasped, taking their bows. The audience is cheering.

I'm too late.

Leo gets his own bow, and when he runs to the front of the stage, I clap along with everyone else, hoping that he might see me in the audience and think I've been here the whole time.

The auditorium lights turn on after that, and everyone streams out to the lobby to congratulate the performers.

I find Beth in the crowd of people.

"Oh, thank goodness," she says when she sees me. "Where were you? I was so worried."

"Sorry," I say, even though I'm not. She has no right to be worried about me. "I was with the support group."

"Next time you should text me, okay?"

"I mean, I'll text my mom," I say, crossing my arms.

People out in the lobby start cheering, and then the cast of the show runs out from the back hallway.

Beth waves her hands over the sea of people, and after a minute Leo finds us.

"Bubs, that was incredible!" She hands him a gift bag and he opens it and pulls out a pack of Reese's. Beth almost never buys outside desserts, except on super special occasions, which I guess this is.

Leo and Beth hug for a long time, then he says, "I'm going back to the changing room," and turns away.

Like he didn't even see me.

"Wait, Leo!" I call out. "You were so good!"

He turns around, and the look he's giving me makes me shrink into myself. "I know you didn't see me perform. Don't even pretend."

He keeps walking toward the changing room, and I run after him.

"I saw your bows!" I say as the shouting in the lobby gets farther and farther away. "Leo, seriously, I didn't mean to miss your opening night. I lost track of the time."

He doesn't respond.

"I *promise* I didn't mean to miss it." I'm jogging to keep up with his fast walk now. DiMeglio would be shocked by the amount of exercise I've gotten today. "I was just with the Bathroom Club, and I lost track of time, and . . ."

He stops and turns around.

"Of course you were with your *support group* friends." He puts his hands on his hips.

"What do you mean?"

"I don't want to talk about this." He keeps walking toward the changing room, but I run to him.

"I really, really wanted to see opening night. I promise." My voice sounds desperate now, and I don't care. "I'll see the other two performances. I'll film them. I'll do whatever!"

"It's not the same. You missed opening night." He tries to walk around me. "You literally don't care about anyone but yourself."

I freeze.

"Um, what?"

"I can't talk about this right now," he says. "We're going to TGI Friday's."

"But you can't just say that and then not talk to me

about it!" I yell at him. "I obviously care about people, are you kidding?"

He looks down. "I'm just saying what I know."

My stomach drops. "What do you know?"

"You don't tell me anything anymore. And my mom told me you still haven't talked to your mom since they told us they're dating. You *only* hang out with people from your support group." He takes a breath. "*That's* what I'm saying."

"Maybe it's because those people actually know what I'm going through."

"AND I DON'T?" Leo shouts. "Al, our moms are dating. They're dating *each other*. I know what you're going through. At least part of it."

"No, you don't."

He rolls his eyes. "You know what, Al? Fine, I don't get it. But you're not the only person with stuff going on."

I clench my jaw. "I know that."

"No, you clearly don't," he says. "Because if you did, then you would've made it to my show."

"I lost track of time!"

"You lose track of everything that doesn't have to do with you!"

"What does that even mean?"

Leo shakes his head. "You haven't checked in on me at all. You haven't asked how *I'm* doing with stuff with our moms. You haven't thought that maybe it would be even harder for me than for you because at least when we go out as a group people might think the three of you are a family." He wipes his hand over his face, wiping away tears that must've just started falling. "You three are tall and pretty and white and could basically be sisters, and I'm short and brown and I just don't fit."

Seeing him cry makes me cry too, no matter how much I don't want to. "Are you serious?" I ask. "Your mom's, like, obsessed with you. My mom even made you grilled cheese. She's *never* done that for me. She doesn't do anything for me except worry."

"That's not true," he says. "She's trying her best."

"How do you know that?" I ask him. I'm being horrible now, but I can't stop it. "How do you know what my mom's doing? She treats me like a *baby* because of my Crohn's."

"You know what, speaking of that, I wasn't gonna say it, but honestly I need to." He takes a breath. "Ever since you found out about being sick, you've been a bad friend."

I try to think of something to say that'll make him see how much that hurts, but all I can do is choke out a sob.

"This was the most important thing I've ever done and you missed it." He puts his hand on the doorknob to the changing room. "We're not siblings, we're not friends, we're not *anything*. Okay?"

Then he walks into the room and slams the door shut.

Chapter Thirty-one

IT ALL COMES OUT (NO, NOT POOP ... WELL, ALSO POOP)

Gym's different without Leo to complain to. And by "different," I mean it's about ten times worse.

It's Tuesday now, and Mr. DiMeglio's forcing us to run again. Anytime I get close to Leo on the track, he jogs ahead. My stomach's gurgling, but I don't stop running. I haven't pooped since Leo and I fought on Sunday, which is probably the longest stretch of time I've ever gone without pooping.

DiMeglio tells us he has a "lunch date at Subway," and lets us leave class a few minutes early. I use that time to run to the locker room bathroom ahead of everyone else, cry, and unleash my severely backed-up bowels.

Everything that I had been holding in comes out—literally—and it hurts so badly that I wish the bald anesthesiologist would knock me out.

I thought getting sick was the worst thing ever, but it really wasn't. It brought me to the Bathroom Club.

But it also took me away from Leo. He's *so* mad at me

right now, which is fair. He doesn't even want to be my friend anymore.

And everything went wrong with Mina too. I shouldn't have even told her I liked her in the first place. I knew it was better to keep it in, to have my queer life separate from my IBD support group life separate from the rest of my life.

After a few minutes and some deep breaths, I wipe my eyes and blow my nose and step out of the stall.

The rest of the day goes downhill after that. My stomach rumbles so loudly that I have to ask to go to the bathroom in almost every single class. Each time is worse than the last.

When I get to math, I try to hold it, but after ten minutes of fidgeting and grabbing my stomach to make sure I don't poop my pants, my teacher tells me to go to the nurse's office, and a few kids who've been in my other classes and seen me ask to go to the bathroom all day giggle.

"I'm fine," I mumble, but then my stomach warns me that it's about to be an emergency, so I run out into the hall.

Instead of going to the nurse's office, I sprint to the nearest bathroom. There's no one in there, so I sit on the toilet and put my head between my knees.

I'm back where I started at the beginning of the school year: one emergency after another. No matter how well the medicine is working, the stress will always get to me. I'll always be the kid who has to run away and poop (or try to).

Maybe I can just do virtual school from the toilet. I'll have my camera off, and I'll learn with the computer on my lap while my feet fall asleep.

At least that way no one would ever see me run into the bathroom again.

But that's impossible, and I don't deserve the peace and quiet anyway.

So, after I finish up, I walk back to class, keep my head down, and try to make it through the rest of the afternoon without Leo.

When the day is finally over, and I'm back at home, I flop into bed, hoodie on, strings tied around my neck so my head is cocooned in the soft fabric.

I didn't talk to anyone for the rest of the day. On the way home, Leo and I walked on opposite sides of the street, pretending not to know each other.

I log out of my backup TikTok. It feels too raw—I don't want anyone to even possibly know that I've had a crush on a girl, that I kissed her, that we were *dating*, and now that's all ruined, along with everything else in my life.

I never posted videos on my backup account, but it used to be the only place I could be openly queer. Even there, though, I never, ever told any of my mutuals about having Crohn's. It's like I have a million secrets and no one in my life knows everything about me. My intestines clench just thinking about it.

There's no one I can talk to. No one knows the entirety of who I am—not Leo, not Mina, not my mom. And I did this to myself.

I pick my phone back up from where I threw it, put in my headphones, and turn the sound all the way up, then I scroll through the For You page on my main TikTok.

"Al?"

I panic and jump off my bed. "Yeah?"

"Can I come in?"

It's Beth. She's outside of my door, in my apartment.

"I know I messed up," I say, loud enough so that she can hear me and hopefully go away. "You don't have to tell me."

"That's not what I was going to say." At that, she opens the door, just a bit. "Can we talk?"

I scramble to pick up all the T-shirts that have respawned out of the T-shirt void. "Fine," I tell her, and she comes in. "But can you close the door?" I don't want my mom over-hearing this conversation, whatever it's going to be.

She does what I ask, then sits at my desk chair. She looks awkward in my room—too tall, too *grown-up*, too . . . Beth—which is kind of nice. At least I get to have this con-versation on my home turf.

Beth leans forward in the chair and clasps her hands together on her knees. When she doesn't say anything for a minute, I tuck my arms into my sweatshirt sleeves and stare down at my comforter. If she's trying to get me to talk first, that's not going to happen.

Finally, she says, "I just wanted to see if you were okay."

"What?" I thought she was going to come here and tell me to make up with my mom and Leo. I thought she'd tell me how terrible I've been to both of them.

"I was telling the truth when I said you could talk to me about anything," she says after a moment. "I want to be someone you can turn to, separate from your mom and Leo."

"How do I know you won't tell them what I say?"

She holds my gaze as she says, "Because I promise you that I won't. And I don't break my promises." She leans forward. "Plus, I'm testing a new recipe, and I need *someone* to try it."

I have to look away, because if I keep staring at Beth, I'm going to cry. She's been there for me since we first moved into this apartment. She's driven me to school and made me a million different baked goods. The only thing that's changed is that now she's my mom's girlfriend.

But maybe, for a few minutes, she can just be Beth again. My neighbor who reminds me so much of my best friend because she's the person who raised him.

"Everything feels like it's my fault." I talk to my comforter, my head down. "I messed things up with my mom. And with Leo."

I want to cry, but I hold it in. Leo's the closest thing I have to a sibling. Even when I'm fighting with my mom, he's there. And saying it out loud makes it real. I don't know if we'll ever come back from this.

"Do you want to talk about it?" Beth asks.

I don't. I don't, I don't, I don't. But when I turn to look at Beth for a second, she's watching me intently, an expression on her face that's something like love.

Plus, I had a scary conversation with Carl and Ethan and I survived. I *more* than survived, actually; I found out that two of my best friends are also queer. I mean, I already know Beth is queer, but still. I remember the relief I felt when I got even just a small thing off my chest.

But if I talk about "it," then I'll have to talk about everything. Not just me being queer, like I did with Carl and Ethan, but all of it.

Maybe that's for the best, though, because I can't keep everything to myself anymore. It's too much; I'll probably explode. At least Beth already knows about me having Crohn's, and she's the one dating my mom, so she obviously knows about that too. I won't have to start from scratch with all the things I've been hiding from the world.

So, finally I say, "Yeah, I do." And then I get into it.

I start with Mina, about how we were dating and how I thought everything was going great until I found out about Beth and my mom. How it felt like the one thing that was *mine* wasn't mine anymore.

"I didn't mean to react the way I did when you told us, but Mina and I had *just* told each other about our feelings, and everything felt new and special. And then you told me that."

Beth nods, but lets me keep talking. So then I tell her about how horrible I feel about what happened with my mom. I tell her about getting into a fight with Mina, and everything leading up to the day of Leo's show. What we said to each other.

I tell the whole story from start to finish, from the first support group meeting until now.

When I'm done, I feel like I just took the biggest poop of my life, like I'm completely empty. There's nothing else in there.

I look up and Beth has tears in her eyes. "Can I come over there?" she asks, and I nod. She rubs my shoulder, and I try not to cry from her touch. "You were holding all of that in, bubs?"

"Like I was constipated for weeks," I say, and Beth smiles.

"Thank you for telling me," she says. "That was really brave."

"It doesn't feel brave." I pull my knees into my chest. "It just feels like I've been mean to so many people."

She moves back to the chair across the room and leans forward again. "You've been going through a lot."

"But so has everyone else," I say. "And I haven't been there for them."

"So, now you can be," Beth insists. "Being in a relationship with someone is an active thing. Whether it's romantic or a friendship or you're in a class with them. It's not just 'that's my friend, end of story.' Every relationship takes work."

When I was diagnosed with Crohn's, my disease was all

I could think about, but now that it's been a little while and my whole life doesn't feel like one big poop-mergency, I can focus on things beyond my stomach. I can actually *show* people I care about them, in a way I haven't been.

"Hey, Beth?" I ask after a minute.

"What's up, bubs?"

"I'm, um . . ." It's not just Leo and Mina who've had to deal with me these past few months. Beth has too. "I'm sorry," I say finally.

"For what?" she asks. "You have *nothing* to be sorry about."

That makes me cry, because I know in a certain sense she's right. Sometimes things are allowed to be hard.

I wipe my eyes and say, "I'm sorry that I was weird around you after I found out you and my mom were dating."

She laughs so gently. "Don't be sorry for that. That was a huge change in your life. I didn't expect you to be totally chill with it right away."

"Yeah, but were you worried that I was, like, mad that my mom was dating a woman?" I don't want her to think that. I never wanted anyone to think that.

She looks thoughtful for a minute and then says, "I could tell you were figuring things out for yourself. And now I get to watch you make it right."

"I will," I tell her, and it feels like a promise.

"I know, bubala," she says. "I know."

Chapter Thirty-two

WE'RE ALL ANXIOUS HERE

I have to ask to go to the bathroom in almost every class the next day. And I don't even care. Because the toilet is where I do my best thinking. I don't notice the people who cycle in and out, talking about their crushes or fixing their mascara or whatever people do in the restroom when they don't have to poop for like half of the day.

After talking to Beth, I've realized how much I've missed Leo and Mina, the two people I talk to the most, the two people I *care* about the most. I pushed them away because I've been too scared to tell them the whole truth, or because I was too focused on my own thing.

I have Crohn's, I like girls, and my mom has a girlfriend.

People are allowed to know this; it's who I am. And if I don't start telling people, I'm going to spend the rest of my life on the toilet being a terrible friend. It felt amazing to tell Beth the whole story, but she's not the only person who needs to know these things.

I guess I always thought that the problem was other

people. That if I told people in my life everything about myself, they'd think I was too much. But the problem was that *I* thought I was too much. And I kind of still do, but, I don't want to. I'm sure that I'm not the only person who's queer and who has a chronic illness and who has a mom who's *also* queer and dating someone.

There are eight billion people in the world or something wild like that. There has to be at least *one* other person.

The only way I'm going to fix things is if I tell people all of it.

Leo and I don't walk home together after school today either, but I don't feel as hopeless as I did yesterday.

As I open the door to the apartment and see my mom sitting on the couch, though, that good feeling fades.

I've been terrible to her. Ever since she told me about Beth, I've been ignoring her, and I've been snapping at her, and I don't want her to think it's because I hate her for being queer, when that couldn't be further from the truth.

She looks over at me and waves a little, then goes back to watching TV. I don't know how to start the conversation we need to have, so I sit on the opposite side of the couch and pretend to watch the show with her.

Eventually, I gather the courage to say *something*. "Why aren't you at work?" I ask after a minute. This is a day where she's almost always scheduled at the grocery store.

She pauses the TV and smiles sadly at me. "I quit."

"What?" I ask. "Because of me? Because of my stomach?"

"No, no," she says, turning toward me. "I just want to take some time and think about what I really want to do."

"Oh," I say, surprised it's not about my stomach for once. "What are you gonna do for work?"

"I'm helping Beth out at the bakery," she says. "But don't worry about me, okay?"

I hate it when she tells me not to worry when that's all I'm good at, and when she's been worrying about me non-stop for months.

"I've actually been trying to find a way to tell you." She sits forward on the couch. "I didn't want you to be stressed out, with everything going on."

"You don't even know what I have going on," I mumble.

"Then tell me, Al," she says forcefully. "I'm not going to know if you don't talk to me."

I shake my head. "You're just gonna say something about my stomach."

"What?" she asks. "What are you talking about?"

I shrug, but I can't stop the tears that well in my eyes, and when my mom sees that I'm crying, *she* starts crying, so then I start crying harder because seeing my mom cry again is the worst thing ever.

"Is this all because of Beth?" she asks.

I shake my head, the tears coming down harder. I don't even know what it's about at this point. There's so much inside of me, and I've been holding it all in.

"How come you didn't tell me that you liked girls?" I ask.

I didn't even know that question was in there, but it seems so obvious. Why didn't she tell me before? Why was the first I heard about it when she started dating Beth?

She looks around the living room, then takes a deep breath. "It didn't seem important," she says. "But I know it was. It is."

"When did you figure it out, though?"

"That I'm bisexual?" she asks, and I want to bury myself under the blankets on the couch and never come out. It's so weird hearing my mom say that. The only people I know who are bi are Rikako and people on TikTok and YouTube.

I nod.

"Is that what you're sad about? Is it about me?" she asks after a minute. She's crying even harder now, and I don't know how to comfort my mom.

"No," I say through tears.

"Can you tell me what it is?" she asks. "I'm worried about you, Al."

I know, I think. *You've been worried about me since I first told you my stomach was hurting. Since the day I was born, probably.*

But instead of saying that, I take a deep breath. My body is cold and numb and I'm going to spend the next week straight on the toilet. But I need to tell her.

"I like girls too." I'm shaking now, but I keep going. "Um, yeah. That's it, I guess. I like girls. And I only like girls, or, like, people who aren't boys. I think I'm a lesbian."

And then my mom does something that she hasn't done in a long, long time: She scoots over on the couch and wraps me in her arms.

I nuzzle into her, and I know I'm getting her shirt soaked in tears, but I also know she doesn't care.

"Why didn't you tell me sooner?" she asks after we've cried for a good long while. "Especially after you knew I was dating Beth? I would never be mad at you for something like that. I'm honestly excited."

The tears start up again, harder this time. "That's the problem."

"That I'm excited?"

I nod and look away from her as I say, "It's *embarrassing*. And I know that sounds bad, but it is." I wipe my eyes with my sleeve and try to explain myself. "I wish I didn't think this way, but it's so weird that we like the same people. That I could talk to you about girls and you'd actually understand." I hiccup, then turn to her. "People already think we're the same, and now we both like girls. It's mortifying."

"Al," my mom says, her voice breaking. "People won't think that. You've never been like me."

I shimmy out of her arms. "What?"

She smiles a little. "I guess that's not exactly what I meant." She puts a hand on my shoulder. "I just mean that you're the most unique kid on earth. You're completely your own person. You're kind and contemplative and mature and playful and I can't believe that I had any part in creating you."

I bury myself into her chest again and sob, because that was exactly what I needed to hear.

After a minute I sit up and wipe my eyes. There's something else I need to tell her.

"Mom?"

"Yeah, Al?"

"I'm not ashamed of you." I squeeze my arms around myself. "I should've said that before." I take a deep breath.

My mom pulls away and pushes a strand of hair behind my ear. "I know, Allie. And it shouldn't be your job to reassure me of that. You're twelve, you're allowed to hate me a little bit."

"I don't hate you," I tell her. "I promise. It's just . . . it's really hard for me when you worry about me all the time. Like, when you tell me what I should eat and stuff like that."

"You're right," she says, and I'm so surprised that I don't know what else to say.

But after a minute I manage to get out "What?"

"I worry about you all the time," she tells me, tears shining in her eyes. "But that doesn't mean I need to show you that worry."

"Oh," I say. It's what I've wanted her to say for so long, but now I can't even form words.

"So, you know how you take medicine every day for your Crohn's?" my mom asks.

"Um, yeah?"

"Well, I take a pill every day for anxiety." She pulls her sleeve down over her hand, which is something that I do too. Especially when I'm nervous. "I'm sorry I haven't talked about this more with you, but I have pretty bad anxiety. Lots of people do. And I take medicine so that I'm less anxious, but it doesn't always work. Especially when there's something that makes me even more anxious than usual."

"Like me?"

"No," she says firmly. "Not *you*. Just what you were going through. I was worried about you, and I didn't know what I could do to help. You're my baby. I never want to see you in pain." She grabs a box of tissues from across the room and pulls one out for herself. "And I know I said we're not the same person—and we're really not—but sometimes this kind of thing can run in families. So, if you have feelings like this, like if you feel anxious or stressed, or anything like that, *please* tell me, okay? Or if you don't want to tell me, tell Dr. Maltz. She might be your gastroenterologist, but I promise you she wants to hear about your brain too. Maybe we can even look into finding you a therapist."

I nod. It still feels weird to tell my mom so much, but it's nice to know I can. That she wants to know. Especially since I *have* had those feelings. A lot. Like, all the time.

"Can I say one more thing?" I ask.

"Of course."

"I'm sorry about how I've been with Beth. Like, how I've been kind of mean to her. But the two of us talked and things are gonna be better. It's just that, like, I didn't really want another mom—one is enough."

My mom snorts at that, then reaches out and smooths my hair. "No one's saying she has to be your mom, Al. But it's never a bad thing to have more people who care about you and love you."

I nod, and I'm crying again. Because of course.

"She can just be your . . . Beth. But she's going to love you, and you can't stop her." My mom laughs. "She already loves you so much."

"I know." And I really do. She feeds me the best foods, and wants to know how my day is, and calls me her bubs.

"You don't just have to have me, you know? You can have Beth, and Leo, and your support group. All of these people love you, and want the best for you. That's the most important thing."

She hands me a tissue, and I blow my nose so loudly it's like a trumpet.

"You *definitely* don't get that from me," my mom says, and we both laugh.

After a minute, I stand up to go. "I love you," I tell her.

She puts a hand to her heart. "I love you too, Al," she says. "More than anything in the whole world."

Chapter Thirty-three

SERGEANT ANCHOVY'S BUTT IS VERY SENSITIVE

"*I now call* this emergency meeting of the Bathroom Club to order," I say.

Ethan laughs. "Hey, that's my thing."

"I know," I say. "I'm stealing it, sorry. But it really is an emergency."

We're at Carl's house now like we had planned earlier in the week, and Ethan was free, so we invited him too. But it's not the full Bathroom Club because Mina's not here. She said it was because she had to study for an earth science test, but I know it's because of me. I don't even know what I would've done if she'd showed up. I need to talk to her one-on-one.

But first, I have to talk to the rest of the Bathroom Club.

The Bathroom Club knows I have Crohn's, and they know about me being queer, but they don't know about my mom and Beth, and I want to tell them.

It's wild how quickly they became some of my best friends in the world. And it's not just because we all have IBD (and we're all queer).

I sit down and pick up Sergeant Anchovy for moral support. He nuzzles my arm and purrs, then flops on my legs.

"Don't touch his butt or he'll bite you," Carl tells me.

Ethan snorts, then reaches out to try to high-five Anchovy's paw. "Same, dude."

And that's what does it, Ethan's silly joke. These are my friends; they're going to understand.

I take a deep breath, then manage to say, "I have to tell all of you something."

"Are you coming out again?" Rikako asks, and everyone laughs, even me.

"No," I say after a minute. It's something else.

I stare down at Sergeant Anchovy, and he meows and head butts me in encouragement, so I start talking. I tell them about my mom and Beth, about how I felt terrible that I didn't tell them, especially when they were all being open and honest about their parents.

"Wait, your mom is dating Leo's mom?" Rikako asks after a minute. When I look up, she's grinning.

"Yeah, she is."

Rikako jumps up, which makes Anchovy jump up too. "That's so cool! Now it's kind of like you and Leo are siblings."

I smile back at them, because it *is* cool. And I've been too caught up worrying about my own stuff to see that.

"I wish my best friend could be my sibling," Ethan says.

"Good thing mine is," Carl announces, and we all turn to

stare at him. "What? Anchovy's my younger brother. We both have diarrhea and we love to sleep."

Ethan shoves Carl and they both fall on the floor laughing. Anchovy moves from my lap and stretches his front paws, then settles down in the middle of all of us.

There's no more tightness in my chest, like I might say the wrong thing or reveal all my secrets.

And honestly, the more I think about it, maybe it wasn't having Crohn's or dealing with my mom that was making me anxious and sad and embarrassed.

Maybe it was me.

Or, like, how I felt about myself.

"Thank you," I say once everyone calms down.

"For what?" Rikako asks.

"For being so welcoming," I tell them.

"What's the Bathroom Club for?" Ethan asks.

"Exactly," I say, remembering what I talked about with Beth. "And I want you to know that I'm here for all of you too. Whenever."

"Same," Carl says. "And Sergeant Anchovy is too."

"Meow," Sergeant Anchovy says.

Rikako puts her hand over Ethan's, then Carl puts his over Rikako's, and I put mine over Carl's.

"'Bathroom Club forever,' on three," Ethan says.

He counts down, and we all shout BATHROOM CLUB FOREVER and throw our arms into the air.

It's cheesy, but it's not embarrassing or anything.

I should've known that they'd be there for me, no questions asked. That I'd always have the Bathroom Club because they already understand a huge part of me.

But really, when it comes down to it, it's just nice to be part of the group.

Chapter Thirty-four

MATEYS FOR LIFE

I've barely spoken to Leo at all since the show. I have so much to apologize for, but I keep chickening out. The stakes are so high with Leo.

Plus, it's easier than you'd think to avoid someone who lives in the same apartment complex as you. You just have to stick to your unit.

But I'm not going to do that today.

I walk across the hall and knock on Leo's front door, but when I try the knob, it's unlocked, so I step in. Normally I'd just barge into Leo's room, but I know he doesn't want me there. So, I knock.

I even do our special knock that we practiced for when we have to tell each other something but we don't want our moms to hear. It's Morse code for *SOS*.

There's nothing for a minute, and then Leo knocks back in Morse code *No*.

Maybe it's worse than I thought.

I take a deep breath and I knock back. *Please?*

But before I'm even done with the word, he opens the door, and I trip forward into his room.

He crosses his arms and sits back on his bed. I stand awkwardly.

"Hey," I say tentatively.

"Hey."

With the comfort that at least he's talking to me, I take a deep breath and blurt out what I came here to say: "Leo, I'm so, so, so, so, so, so sorry."

He stares at me for a second, a look in his eyes I've never seen before. "For what?"

Leo deserves an explanation for why I've acted the way I have, but knowing what I need to say doesn't make it any easier to start.

"For missing your show," I say, and he doesn't uncross his arms. "And for being selfish and mean about our moms and for not thinking about how you were feeling and for not telling you everything that's going on with me." I look down at my shoes. "And also for being jealous when you go over to your dad's house. I know how important his side of the family is to you and I shouldn't have felt like that."

"You were jealous?"

I nod. "You have such a cool dad and you have a whole other side of your family who loves you and who cook you amazing food and who want to see you. I know I shouldn't be jealous, but sometimes I am."

He uncrosses his arms. "It's okay if you're jealous of me," he says, and there's a hint of a smile in his voice. "I'm amazing."

I want to laugh, but I don't know if I should. I still don't know if he's going to forgive me.

Then he stands up and wraps me in a hug. "Thanks for saying all that, Al."

I squeeze him super tightly and nod so he knows I heard him.

When we pull apart, he says, "Plus, I need to apologize too. I should've told you I wanted to do drama club sooner. I've wanted to do it for a long time. And I know I've been hanging out with Peregrine a lot."

I shrug. "It's okay. *I* was hanging out with the Bathroom Club a lot."

But I'm still nervous. There's so much more that I need to tell him.

He's the only person I want to talk to about *everything* that happened with Mina, and he doesn't even know I'm queer.

I move to sit next to him on his bed and stare down at his dark blue comforter. "There's actually something else I need to apologize for."

"Um, okay?" he says, raising his eyebrows. "Can you just say it? You're kind of scaring me."

"It's nothing bad."

"What is it, then?" he asks, concern in his voice.

"You know Mina?" I ask. "My friend from the support group?"

"Yeah, of course."

"We were kind of . . . dating."

I bite my lip and squeeze my eyes shut, then open them. When I do, Leo's staring at me, mouth open.

"Wait, you were *dating* Mina?" He forces his mouth closed with a hand. "More importantly, *were*? Like, not anymore?"

"Well, yeah. We kind of broke up."

He grins. "So, you're, like, a lesbian?"

I shrug. "Yeah, I think so." He's still giving me a weird look. "Why are you staring at me like that?"

"Al," he says, jumping onto his knees and bouncing a little on the bed. "I'm gay."

Now it's my turn for my mouth to open.

"Don't act surprised," he says. "I thought you knew."

"WHAT?" I shout, then a little quieter, "What? Why'd you think that??"

"Because, like, I didn't really think I was trying to hide it." He shrugs. "I just thought it was kind of obvious."

"It wasn't!" I tell him. Though maybe it's just that I wasn't paying enough attention to him this year.

"Come on," he says. "Even my mom knows."

"WHAT?" I shout again.

"I told her a while ago, the night we got home from seeing *Wicked*." He stands up on the bed and then jumps off of it, sitting down on the carpet. "I told her in private because I wanted it to be special. I *honestly* thought you knew."

"Leo, I literally didn't know. Otherwise I would've told you about me."

He slaps his hand to his head dramatically. "This is a classic case of miscommunication," he says. "Like in a Shakespeare play."

I join him on the floor and shove him. "Just because you do drama club now, you're somehow the Shakespeare expert?"

"I mean, I've seen *The Lion King*," he says. "And that's based on *Hamlet*, so . . ."

I shove him again, and he hug-tackles me so we're both lying down. "I also just wanted to say I'm sorry if you thought I was mad about our moms dating because I was, like, homophobic or something."

"I didn't think that," he says. "Honestly, I didn't know what was happening."

"It's just that after my mom came out, I didn't want to tell people I like girls too because I thought it would be too embarrassing."

"I don't think people will be mean about it or anything," Leo says. "But they might be confused now if we tell them that every single person in our family is queer. Not that that's our problem, it's just kind of funny."

I feel warm when Leo says "our family."

"So, what happened with you and Mina?" he asks when I don't respond for a beat. "How come you're not dating anymore?"

"It's nothing," I say. But he tilts his head and raises his eyebrows in a way that says *It's absolutely* not *nothing,* so I add, "We had a fight. I tried to hide our relationship from our moms, and she didn't understand why I wanted to do that. But either way, she doesn't want anything to do with me."

"I'm sure that's not true."

I shrug, which is hard to do while lying down.

But then I sit up when I realize something.

"Wait, so are you and Peregrine, like, dating?" I ask. "I mean, I know him and Mina met at the queer youth center, so . . ."

"No," Leo says quickly. "Well, not that I don't *want* us to be. But we're not."

"Do you have a crush on him?"

Leo nods. "Oh my god, yes."

I laugh. "Then *tell him!*" I say excitedly. "Then we can both be dating someone."

I say it before I remember that Mina and I aren't dating anymore. That I ruined everything.

"Maybe I will," Leo says, smiling.

But things are a thousand times better with Leo now. And I want our friendship to be an active thing, to show him I care about him every day. So I ask, "Would you want to have a sleepover tonight?"

"Duh," he says. "But on one condition: Since you're making me talk to Peregrine, *you* need to talk to Mina."

I shake my head. "I don't think she wants to talk to me."

"How do you know?"

"We got into a fight."

"So? We did too. And now we're not in a fight anymore."

That makes it sound so easy. Obviously, Leo and I aren't in a fight anymore: We're family. But Mina's just some girl who I kissed once.

"Al, please?" he asks, bringing out his puppy dog eyes.

I put my head in my hands. "Ugh. Fine."

He grins at me. "Then I'm in. I'd be in no matter what. I'll never turn down a sleepover."

"Leo?" I ask.

"Al?"

"You're my best friend in the whole world."

"Obviously," he says.

"And maybe it's kind of like . . ." I take a breath. "Maybe it's kind of like you're my brother."

He sits up and grins. "Definitely," he says. "And you're my annoying little sister."

I scoff and pretend I'm super hurt by that. "You're only three months older than me."

"And three months wiser."

I roll my eyes. "Sure, sure."

After that, we watch some *High School Musical: The Musical: The Series* together on his phone, and I finally tell him that I think Olivia Rodrigo and JoJo Siwa are cute (since we're watching the episode where JoJo guest stars), and *he* finally tells me that he thinks Joshua Bassett is cute, and we both laugh at that, and it's perfect.

I don't know why I was ever scared to tell him anything. I feel so much lighter now, it's ridiculous.

"Ecretsay andshakehay?" I ask when the episode's over, and Leo nods solemnly.

We do the double high five that starts the handshake, then grab each other's hands, cross them, and release them with an explosion sound.

"Al," Leo says, pointing to me.

"Leo," I say, pointing to him.

We wrap our bent index fingers around each other. "Arrrr! MATEYS FOR LIFE!"

When we say it this time, it feels truer than ever.

Chapter Thirty-five

A PROCLAMATION OF LIKE

My mom drives me over to Mina's house when I tell her what I want to do.

"Ooh, this is so exciting," she says. "A proclamation of love."

I roll my eyes. "Mom, gross, no."

But that's kind of what I'm planning.

I mean, not love—that's too much. But I want to tell Mina that I still like her. I want us to *talk*. Because as it turns out, telling people how you're feeling is actually . . . good? And my stomach hurts less than it has in a long time.

Who knew?

"Is this her house?" my mom asks.

I nod, and my mom parks the car.

"What if she doesn't want to talk?" I ask, more to myself than my mom.

"Then at least you tried," she says. "But I really think she'll at least want to hear what you have to say."

I shrug. "Hopefully."

My mom reaches over and smooths out my hair, then licks one of her fingers and rubs something off of my cheek, like she did when I was little and dirty from playing outside for too long.

"Oh my god, Mom, that's so disgusting."

"Sorry, sorry," she says, but she's smiling.

I pull out my phone to text Mina.

ME: hey
im outside

I wait a minute to see if she'll respond, but then it's five minutes, then ten minutes, then twenty.

"Maybe you should knock on the door," my mom says, which makes my stomach go wild.

I hate knocking on doors. Especially when they might get slammed in my face.

But after another five minutes and no response, I get out of the car and slowly make my way up the front walk.

I turn around, and my mom is giving me a thumbs-up from the car. I roll my eyes at her and then smile as I turn back to face the door.

Just as I'm about to knock, though, there's a loud noise from the foyer.

It sounds like people fighting.

I back away from the door and turn to look at my mom to see if she's hearing it too, but she's checking her phone.

Part of me wants to go back to the safety of my mom's car, but then I get a text from Mina.

MINA: ok

That's all she says, *ok*, but it feels like hope.

A few minutes later, Mina comes out, her face streaked with tears. Now that the door is open, I can hear that the loud noise is from her parents fighting.

She starts walking down the sidewalk, away from her house, and I run a little to catch up with her.

"I know you're probably mad at me," I start. "But do you want to come over to my apartment for a little while?" I nod over to where my mom has the car parked.

Mina looks too, then she glances back at her house.

"Okay," she says, staring at the ground. "Fine, yeah. Thanks."

We walk over to the car, and my mom unlocks the door.

"Hi, Mina," my mom says as we climb into the back. "Do you want me to go tell your parents you're coming over?"

Mina nods and wipes at her eyes, and my mom jogs over to the open door of her house. Mina and I are silent the whole time, but once my mom gets back, she gives a thumbs-up.

"They gave the go-ahead," my mom says gently. "You can even sleep in our apartment tonight if you want, okay?"

Mina nods, and right as she snaps the buckle on her seat belt, my mom drives off.

Chapter Thirty-six

CHOCOLATE CHIP COOKIES AND CROHN'S TIKTOKS

"This hot chocolate can't cure *everything*," Beth says to Mina, who's wearing some of my pajamas (which I'm trying not to be embarrassed about considering the fact that she didn't bring any overnight clothes). "But it can definitely help."

Beth hands Mina a giant steaming mug of freshly made hot chocolate covered in whipped cream and topped with chocolate shavings. Then she hands me and Leo smaller mugs of the same.

"Thanks," Mina says, smiling a little.

We haven't talked about anything that's happened between us yet, but I'm glad Mina's over here. I know sometimes her parents get into really big fights, but it was kind of scary to hear one in person.

And once Mina gets some hot chocolate in her, she's somewhat back to her normal self. Personally, I'm trying really hard not to feel awkward, even though the girl I was dating—and, fine, definitely still have a crush on—is sitting here in my living room, drinking out of my mug and wearing my pajamas.

"Do you wanna go watch a movie or something?" I ask her after we're done with our hot chocolate.

"Can I come?" Leo asks, but I give him a look, and he must get the message, because he says, "Actually, never mind, I have to do some, uh, homework or something."

Mina follows me into my bedroom, and I don't close the door even though my mom didn't say that I had to leave it open. It just feels better, for me and for her.

We watch a few minutes of *Lilo & Stitch*, with Mina on the bed and me on the floor, but when I turn around to check on her, there are tears in her eyes, and it isn't even a sad part. Lilo's just feeding peanut butter and jelly sandwiches to the fish.

"Are you okay?"

She shakes her head as she wipes away some of the tears and snot. I sit next to her on the bed, though I don't know if it's okay for me to give her a hug or even pat her shoulder or anything. But then she lays her head in my lap, and I stroke her curly hair as she cries. My chest feels warm and sad and happy and a thousand different things, but none of the feeling travels down to my intestines. Maybe it's because these are feelings everyone has, not just kids with chronic illnesses.

I don't know what to say to make her feel better, but I want to start with the truth, at least.

"I'm sorry about not telling my mom and Beth that we were dating." She sniffles and looks up at me as I say it. "I just hated the idea that they'd think about me differently, and that maybe everyone would think I was just copying them and that I didn't really like you."

This makes her laugh, and it's an incredible sound. "Al, I could tell you liked me."

"Oh, yeah?"

She nods. "Yeah. You made it pretty obvious."

"Good," I say. And then quieter: "I still do."

She looks down. "I still like you too."

We don't say anything for a minute, but finally, Mina says, "My parents have been fighting way more. I don't even know what's happening most of the time, but they're both trying to get custody of me and my brother, and it's kind of messy."

"I'm sorry," I say, because I really, truly am.

"And I just loved being in your apartment and hanging out with you and Leo and seeing your mom and Beth being girlfriends." She takes a shaky breath. "It kind of felt like I was a part of your family for a little while."

"Really?"

She nods, and now *I'm* tearing up. I never thought that the weird little two-apartment family made up of my mom and Beth and Leo and me would be something that would make someone jealous.

But I guess I *am* lucky to have them.

After that, we watch the rest of *Lilo & Stitch* while Mina tells me about some animals that only live in Hawaii, like the pueo, which is a short-eared owl. She stays in my lap the whole time, and I can't stop grinning at her.

When the movie's done, we head out to the living room, where Beth and Leo and my mom are watching a reality show about glass blowing. My mom's arm is on Beth's knee, and Leo is leaning against his mom's shoulder. For the first time, seeing them sitting like this doesn't make me mad. I want to sit with them too. I want to be a part of the family.

"Hey," my mom says, smiling at Mina. "You need anything? Water? A snack? Pizza?"

"Um, no thanks," Mina says.

Beth pauses the TV and sits up. "But you know what we *do* need?"

"What?" Leo asks, jumping up to stand next to me and Mina.

"We need a baking party."

"YES!" Leo shouts, grinning.

"Come on, kinder," Beth says. "Let's go downstairs and grab the ingredients."

Mina looks over at me and smiles a little, and I smile back at her. We all head down to the bakery in our pajamas, which feels silly but it's so fun. Beth turns on the work lights and hands us chocolate chips and butter and all the ingredients we need to make her famous chocolate chip cookies.

When she tosses us the bag of flour, it spills a little, and we get flour on our faces and hands.

"We'll clean it up tomorrow," Beth says with a wink, then throws flour in Leo's face. Leo throws some at me, and after that Mina grabs a handful and chucks it at me as well, and soon I'm covered in a pile of flour. I giggle and take two handfuls from the industrial bag and throw one at Leo and one at Mina.

I must let my guard down for a second too long, though, because when I'm not looking, my mom sneaks up behind me and sprinkles even more flour on my hair before wrapping me in a hug.

"I love you, kid," she whispers in my ear.

"I love you too," I tell her.

We head back upstairs to make the cookies in Beth's oven. We all help with something: My mom browns the butter, I measure out the dry ingredients, Leo stirs everything together, and Mina portions out the cookies onto the baking sheet. While we're waiting for them to bake, we play Sushi Go! as my mom cooks dinner, and I finally win a round (just before Mina beats all of us).

"Taste this," my mom says to Beth, shoving a spoonful of something into her face. She's been "cooking" for the past few hours, letting ingredients simmer in Beth's kitchen.

Beth sniffs it and takes a hesitant bite. "Wow, babe, this is . . ."

My mom laughs and calls me over. "Al, come on, try it. It can't be *that* bad."

She grabs another spoon out of the drawer and I try some of whatever my mom made. The fact that she's cooking at all must be Beth's influence, which seems good, until I take a bite.

"Mmm," I say, but the wince must give me away.

"Okay, so, maybe it's not Beth level," my mom says, grabbing the spoons from the two of us. "But at least I'm trying."

"I don't mind cooking, you know," Beth tells my mom.

"Yeah, can you *please* just let Beth cook?" I ask, and Beth gives me a thumbs-up behind my mom's back.

My mom points between me and Beth. "Did you pay her to say that?"

Leo and Mina laugh from the table. "I'm sure it's not *that* bad," Leo says. Then he comes over and tastes it.

Mina tries it too, and the three of us are all coughing and pretending like my mom poisoned us or something.

"How about this," Beth says. "I'll cook us dinner, and when I can't, we'll just order takeout?"

We all agree that that's the perfect plan, and I get kind of excited thinking about how most nights we're going to have dinner together.

As a family.

And maybe Mina can come by too, and we won't have to hide anything and I won't be ashamed.

We decide to skip dinner and just eat the cookies, but before we do, Leo clears his throat.

"Attention everyone," he shouts, slightly too loud for the small room.

"We can all hear you," Mina says, covering her ears and laughing. "We're right here."

"Fine, fine," he says with a wave of his hand. "But listen, Al and I have something to show you all."

My mom and Beth and Mina turn to face us, and I grin. "Be right back!" A minute later, I'm standing next to Leo, tuning my ukulele.

"Count us in, Al," Leo says, turning around and giving me a thumbs-up.

I grin at him. It's our first time performing together in front of someone other than our moms, and I can't wait.

And not only that.

It'll be my first time *singing*. I promised Leo we'd do it together, and this time I'm not going back on my word. We planned it all out last night.

"FIVE, SIX, A FIVE SIX SEVEN EIGHT!"

I strum the first chords of the song, and Leo and I start to belt it out. It's a parody we came up with the other night of "Drivers License."

I got my diagnosis last week
Just like we always talked about
'Cause I do way too much pooping
And now I have to figure it out

When we're done, our moms and Mina give us a standing ovation, and Beth passes out the cookies. It's perfect.

"These are the best cookies I've ever tasted in my entire life," Mina says.

Beth grins at her. "See, bubs," she says to Leo. "They really are the best."

"Yeah, yeah," Leo says.

"He likes the packaged kind better," I stage-whisper to Mina, and everyone laughs.

When we're done with dessert, Leo grabs a sleeping bag and an air mattress, and he sets us up for a sleepover in his room.

We play truth or dare and then talk about our favorite movies and books and games and how we wish more people in our town would come out as queer in middle school so that we weren't alone.

"I'm gonna go empty my bag," Mina says after a little while.

"Your bag?" Leo asks, confused, and I explain all about colostomy bags to him as Mina goes to the bathroom. It's cool to be the one in the know for once, especially about my own illness.

When she comes back, I pull out my phone. "The Bathroom Club wants to FaceTime," I tell her.

"Oh," Leo says, looking down. "I can go hang out in the living room."

"What?" I ask. "No way, we're *all* FaceTiming."

I prop my phone on Leo's nightstand so that the three of us are in the frame.

"Hey, Leo!" Rikako says from their little square.

Leo introduces himself to everyone, and then we all decide to play Among Us.

"You should invite Peregrine to play with us too," I whisper to Leo after a couple of rounds.

"No way," he whispers back.

"You really should," Mina sing-songs.

So Leo sends him a text, and a few minutes later Peregrine is on the group FaceTime too, beating us all at Among Us and making Leo laugh.

After a while the people on the FaceTime have to go to bed, but Mina and Leo and I aren't tired.

"Let's make a TikTok," I say, grinning conspiratorially.

"Okay . . ." Leo says.

"We could do one that's like a put a finger down challenge," I suggest. "Like, put a finger down, Crohn's edition."

It's the first time I've ever wanted to post about Crohn's on TikTok (or post anything at all). But I need everyone to know every part of my life, even people who only know me from my alt TikTok.

"And put a finger down, queer middle-schooler edition," Leo suggests.

"Ooh, yeah," I say. "We can do both."

Leo pulls his phone out. "I'll film the Crohn's one, since that's your thing."

Mina and I agree, and we whisper about what we'll say for the challenge, and then we have Leo film it.

"Okay," I say, already giggling. It's weird being in front of the camera talking about poop, but I kind of love it. Especially with Mina next to me. "Put a finger down if you've ever farted in class and then blamed it on someone else."

I put my finger down right away, because I've done that (whoopsie), and after a second Mina puts her finger down too, and we all burst out laughing.

When we're done with that, we film one about being queer in middle school that Leo joins in on too.

It's amazing to be able to talk so openly about these things with the two people who know me best. To double post it on my main and my backup TikTok. People at school can see it. I actually kind of *want* them to see, especially the one with Mina and Leo.

We get ready for bed soon after that, with Mina and me on Leo's floor in sleeping bags. When Leo turns the lights off, Mina scoots her sleeping bag as close as possible to mine.

Just before I'm about to drift off, Mina turns on her side and whispers to me, "I'm so lucky."

"What?" I smile. "Why?"

She wiggles an arm out of her sleeping bag and gently shoves my shoulder. "Because you're my girlfriend."

I grin. "Yeah? Even though we got into a fight?"

"Definitely. Girlfriends can fight, but I'm glad we made up." She takes a breath and whispers, "And because of how nice your family was to me today."

"Of course," I say.

She leans in and kisses my forehead, and my face gets hot and I bury it into my sleeping bag and almost scream with joy (but I don't so that I don't wake up Leo).

Then we fall asleep, side by side, cozy in Leo's bedroom. Everyone I care about is under this one roof, in an apartment above a Jewish bakery, in a place where I can be completely myself—whoever that turns out to be.

ACKNOWLEDGMENTS

I wrote and revised most of this book on my home toilet, so my first thank-you has to go to her. You're a star!

Thank you to my incredible editor, Ellen Cormier, who always finds the heart of my stories and helps me yank them out into the world. And to Squish Pruitt, who was not only one of the first readers, but has been so instrumental in providing feedback throughout this whole editorial process. I'm so happy to have you on the team!

A million thanks would not be enough to properly express my gratitude to my agent, Jim McCarthy, who is my staunchest advocate and who has fought the whole way to maintain the poopy heart of this story.

Thank you to everyone at Dial/Penguin who had a hand in bringing this book out into the world: Jen Klonsky, Nancy Mercado, Cerise Steel, Regina Castillo, Tabitha Dulla, Emily Romero, Christina Colangelo, Bri Lockhart, Danielle Presley, Alex Garber, Lauren Festa, Tolani Osan, Carmen Iaria, Trevor Ingerson, Summer Ogata, Rachel Wease, Shanta Newlin, and Elyse Marshall.

Thank you in particular to Venessa Carson and Judith Huerta, who helped me tremendously at my first ever conference and who are two of the hardest working people I've ever met.

Thank you to the cover artist of my DREAMS, Aishwarya Tandon, who has been most supportive and who is wildly talented! And thank you to my cover designer, Kaitlin Yang, whose toilet-based intuition is clearly inspired.

Thank you to my entire gastroenterological care team throughout my life. You have always made me feel comfortable and cared for even when things felt terrifying. And now that I'm responsible for my own care, I have to thank my mom about one million times over, because I know how impossible it is to get doctors on the phone and to deal with insurance. Thank you for coordinating . . . all of that, and for taking me to appointments and for everything.

Thank you to Zachy, who is the exact same age as Al and most of the kids in the book. I hope I did an okay job at representing what it's like to be a seventh grader. Love you!!!!!

Thank you to every writing friend who has comforted me, lied to me, and told me what I want to hear. You know who you are.

Thank you to Louisa for the chapter title.

Always and forever thank you to Ana, Gru, Len, Sal, Sab & Zar. I would pick up (and have picked up) FaceTimes from the toilet for all of you.

To Daniela and Flan, my roommates and loves. Thank

you to Fry for keeping me company when I stay up late to write, and to Daniela for welcoming me back into bed when I'm done.

And to everyone at CCFA's Camp Oasis. Thank you for providing me a space to be a kid with Crohn's, to go to camp, to learn about myself and my disease. This book wouldn't have happened without all of you.

Dear Reader,

Like Al, I was diagnosed with Crohn's in middle school, and I don't think that was a coincidence. I was going through puberty, or whatever version of it I could muster as my body waged a war against itself. I was also making and losing friends and learning what I had to do to fit in when I had never even thought to do so before. My stomach responded to these changes and my anxiety with blood and pain and so much poop.

Puberty is hard enough, but when you add a chronic illness that takes place mostly in the bathroom to an already mortifying process, it becomes unbearable. If you're going through this right now, please just know that you will make it out. Middle school is not forever, no matter how much it may feel like it.

When your body is both changing and fighting you, it can feel like the end of the world. Unlike Al, I didn't know that I was queer in middle school, but if I had read stories like hers, maybe it would've helped me not feel so out of place. Because I wasn't, and you're not, whoever you are. I thought when I wrote this book that a character being chronically ill AND queer AND Jewish would be too much, but I'm all three of those things and I am exactly the right amount.

If you're a grown-up reading this to try to understand your chronically ill (and/or queer) kid better, please internalize the following words: We know when we're hurting. We know how we feel. And, as much as you might wish it can, your worry cannot fix us, because we don't need to be fixed.

Here are some resources that I encourage both kids and grown-ups to check out. They exist for a reason, so please don't feel any shame using them. That's literally what they are there for:

- Crohn's and Colitis Foundation's "Find a Support Group" feature to find your own Bathroom Club! https://www.crohnscolitisfoundation.org/find-a-support-group
- Crohn's & Colitis Foundation's Camp Oasis (a week-long camp specifically for kids with IBD!)
- The "We Can't Wait" app to help you locate accessible public restrooms
- The Trevor Project for queer youth—you can even text them at 678-678